D0004485

achimoona

achimoona

introduced by Maria Campbell

FIFTH HOUSE
SASKATOON, SASKATCHEWAN
1985

Copyright ©1985 the authors

All rights reserved. No part of this book may be reproduced in any form or by any means, electronic or mechanical, without permission in writing from the publisher, except by a reviewer, who may quote brief passages in a review to print in a magazine or newspaper or broadcast on radio or television.

Canadian Cataloguing in Publication Data

Main entry under title:
Achimoona
ISBN 0-920079-16-4
1. Children's stories, Canadian (English) – Indian authors.* 2. Canadian fiction (English) – 20th century.*
PS8321.A29 1985   jC813'.01'08   C85-091247-4
PZ5.A29 1985

Thanks to the following for their assistance in the preparation of this book: Saskatchewan Education, Indian and Metis Curriculum Advisory Committee, Gabriel's Crossing Foundation, Stan Cuthand, Beth Cuthand.

To Smith Atimoyoo and Stan Cuthand
for their support and encouragement

ki na nas koom tinan

This book has been published with the assistance of:
Secretary of State Canadian Studies Program
The Canada Council
Saskatchewan Arts Board

Published by
Fifth House
406 Clarence Ave. S.
Saskatoon, Saskatchewan
S7H 2C7

Typeset by
Apex Design Graphics
Saskatoon, Saskatchewan

Printed by
Kromar Printing
Winnipeg, Manitoba

CONTENTS

LIST OF ILLUSTRATIONS

Dress for Ara, Easy Afternoon from the collection of the Department of Indian Affairs and Northern Development, Saskatchewan Region
Mystic Moose, Frost Moon, Harvest Moon, Bald Eagle Moon, Hatching Moon from the collection of the Saskatchewan Indian Cultural College
Making My Dad's Tea, Just Visiting from the collection of the Native Heritage Foundation of Canada
remaining works from private collections

about the cover of the book
Hatching Moon *by Raymond McCallum*
Hatching Moon is the time of year when the world awakens from the long sleep of winter. This picture depicts this awakening—both in human and animal terms. Each spring new life emerges to renew the world—plants, animals and insects. The woman and female bird are representative of this renewal, from where all life begins, and they are therefore one of the most important components of the circle of life.

Introduction

Hi!

I am glad you have a copy of our book and I hope you will enjoy the stories. But before you begin reading, I want to tell you a bit about how the stories were born.

I'll bet you never thought stories were born. Well, they are, you know. Just like everything on the earth is born, stories come from thoughts that begin in the mind.

In my language, which is Cree, the mind is called *mom tune ay chi kun.*[1] *Mom tune ay chi kun* is the sacred place inside each one of us where no one else can go. It is in this place that each one of us can dream, imagine, fantasize, create and, yes even talk to the grandfathers and grandmothers.

The thoughts and images that come from this place are called *mom tune ay chi kuna*, which means wisdoms, and they can be given to others in stories, songs, dances and art.

Stories are called *achimoona*, songs are *nugamoona*, dances are *neemeetoona* and art is called *tatsinaikewin*. They sound almost the same, don't they? That is because all these words describe gifts that come from the sacred place inside. But I'm only going to tell you about *achimoona*, stories, because that is what this book is about.

In our old way, *achimoona* were never written down because we are what is known as an oral people, that means we talked, we didn't write. All our history, our legends, our way of believing, everything was passed on to each generation orally. We had people whose job it was to tell stories. They were our teachers and historians and they had a special and important role in our communities.

Storytellers had to spend many years perfecting their craft. They had to spend hours alone in the sacred place thinking and creating new stories and finding the right words and ways to tell them. They also had to apprentice under an old storyteller until they had learned, understood and memorized all of the ancient stories so that they could be passed on to a new generation and not be lost.

As well as learning all of this, they had to learn the rules of storytelling and one of the rules was: storytelling was only done during the winter months and it had to stop when the frogs started to sing in the spring.

Have you ever sat down in the evening when your work is all done and listened to frogs sing or ducks and geese talk?

The whole night is alive with their songs and stories; they soothe us and fill us with strength and purpose. It's very important for us to listen to them because they are our family, too, and among them are great storytellers, who can also teach.

Some people say those are the old ways, but times change, not just for us but for the earth and all her creatures, too. I think the change is not in the sacred place but in the ways that the stories are given.

The oral storytellers still live in our communities and the frogs still sing, but English is slowly becoming our language and hardly anybody lives close to nature anymore, so it's hard to think of frogs, ducks and geese as family, and it's hard to go to that sacred place and express wisdoms in the new language.

Language comes from a people's spiritual and cultural base and so sometimes it is painful for us to use this new language because its base is very different from ours.

Our new storytellers have a big job. They must understand their sacred place and they must also understand the new language and use it to express their stories without losing the thoughts and images that are culturally unique to them. This new storyteller must also be a translator of the old way, so that it will not be lost to a new generation. And all of this must be done on paper, for that is the new way.

The stories you will be reading in this book were written by our new storytellers and the way that these stories came about is a bit different from the way *achimoona* are usually born.

The storytellers and I got together at Gabriel's Crossing and talked for many hours about the things I just told you about. We wanted to write stories for you, and that became a big problem, because, you see, in our culture there is no such thing as stories for young people. *Achimoona* are for everyone. Each person, young or old, finds the things in the story that are meant for him or her. That is one of the special gifts of the oral storyteller—to be able to weave all the lessons, messages or jokes into a story and not leave anyone out.

We also talked about how we could help people understand our culture without giving a big, boring lesson about it. We remembered something that the old ones remind us of all the time and that is the four colours that represent all the things of the earth: black, red, yellow and white. These colours represent the four peoples of the earth, the four directions, the four elements, the four creatures and the four minerals. We are told that all these things are our family and that we all come from and live on mother earth. If we always keep that as our centre we will never lose the spirit of our stories.

Well, we did lots of talking, but we all knew that we had to go to that special place inside of us, the one we call *mom tune ay chi kun*, and try to find a story for you.

Deciding to do that does not mean it just happens. You know how hard it is to make yourself still inside, when your head is full of all kinds of things. So to go there we tried something old—we made a medicine bundle.

I went around the house and the countryside, picked different things and put them in the bag. There were stones, feathers, jewelry, pieces of print cloth, leather, a tea pail, a beaded bag, tobacco, snuff, a book, fish scales. I put the bag in the middle of the room and each storyteller picked something from it. They felt it, looked at it, smelled it, then shut their eyes and let the object tell them a story.

After about half an hour everyone was ready to tell the story they had been given. The stories the objects told were beautiful; they were full of magic and music and they contained answers to many of the questions we had been asking.

Now came the big job, to take those oral stories and put them on paper. It was hard, we had to change from telling a story to a group of people to being alone and telling the story to the paper. Because there are no facilities at Gabriel's Crossing, the storytellers stayed in tents and teepees. We have some photos of the storytellers working at their typewriters in teepees.

Jordon did all his writing on top of a big hill overlooking the river. John did his in a leanto porch. Peter walked all over and found different spots. Bernelda did her writing in a bedroom and Priscilla did hers on a blanket in the sun. Darlene stayed in her tent and Harvey found a spot by the river. The summer was hot and windy. In a way it was like storytellers worked long ago.

Many stories came to each storyteller. The publisher picked these eight stories and one poem for this book, and then picked the art from work already done by Native artists in Saskatchewan.

Remember the word for art? *Tatsinaikewin*. It came from the same place that stories come from.

This is our first collection of contemporary *achimoona*. It has been an exciting and rewarding experience for all of us. Above all, it has been a learning experience and that is really what storytelling is about. To learn from all the things around us and to find a way to give it to others. In our language that is called *magewin*— to give away.

Maria Campbell, Gabriel's Crossing
Batoche, Saskatchewan, March 1985

[1] We have tried to spell the Cree words so that you could all say them the way they sound in Cree.

The Boy and The Eagle

Peter Deranger

"There is something there, I just know it," John Bullmoose was thinking as he walked behind his father.

Harry Bullmoose, John's father, was a Chipewayan Indian trapper living in the wilderness of northern Saskatchewan. This year John had come along to the trapline. They were cutting a supply of wood for the winter. In another week they would have enough, then they could begin to set traps.

It was almost two weeks now since the first snowfall. That's when they had seen the mink tracks by the river just behind their log cabin. The old man had showed his son how to set a mink trap there.

Every day, while his father cut wood, John followed the winding path to the place where the trap was set. Every day there was nothing there.

Today his spine tingled as he walked slowly on the path.

"I'll just be over there, son," Harry said, pointing a few yards from where he had been cutting wood yesterday.

"Okay," John said, "I won't be long."

The path wound around a small hill. He stopped under a tall jackpine. A woodpecker was rattling on a dead tree nearby. A squirrel chattered, and scurried across the path and into the thicket.

A chill hung in the air. There was frost on the willows and on the branches of the black spruce.

From where he was standing, John could see the river. It was moving slowly, trickling over the pebbles and rocks.

He walked as quietly as possible, trying not to disrupt the stillness in the forest. Then he heard it—a shrill squawk. It startled him. It sounded like a cry of pain. John wanted to run back to his father, but he was also very curious. He took a few more steps. There was a movement in the bush behind the rock. There was something caught in the trap. it was too big to be a mink. He picked up a stick just in case.

The first thing he saw was a huge pair of wings, flapping desperately. Steel jaws were locked onto the claws of an eagle. When it saw John, it fought harder than ever. Twigs, feathers and snow flew into the air.

John froze on the spot. He dropped his club. He could not move or make a sound. For a long time the eagle fought to free itself. Then it stopped, and folded its wings. It stood there, trapped, staring at the little boy.

"Wow," John thought after a while, "what a beautiful creature." He remembered something his grandfather had said about eagles one time, but he couldn't really remember what it was. His father had also told him something about finding an animal caught in a trap. "Always make an offering to the spirit of that animal," he had said. "The animal offered himself to us, and we have to be thankful for that." John had some tobacco in his pocket. It was tied in red cloth his father had made for him.

He took out the tobacco and held it in his hand. He looked into the eagle's eyes. It was pain that shone back at him. Suddenly, John could not stand to see the eagle caught in the trap that was not meant for it.

"I'm sorry," John said, "I am going to give you this tobacco. I'll tie it around your leg, then I'll set you free."

The eagle jumped back at first, when the boy came closer, then it stood still once more. John tied the tobacco around its claw, and loosened the spring that locked the trap. The eagle was free. It spread its wings and flew away.

That evening when supper was done, John told his father what had happened. The old man sipped his hot tea and sat very quiet for a moment, then he said, "You did a good thing, my son. The eagle will not forget it."

Two weeks later, cold wind settled over the land and all the little lakes froze. On the fourth morning after the big lake was frozen over, John's father said after breakfast, "Son, we have enough wood now to last awhile. We are going to set traps today. Along the shore, the lake is hard enough, but out there, there are still some soft parts. So we'll have to stay along the shore."

John was happy to be going out. "Can we put Wolfy on the harness, papa? He can pull me on my sleigh."

"Well, I don't know," the old man hesitated.

"Please, daddy," John could hardly wait to go on the first sleigh ride of the early winter.

"Well, all right," his father agreed, "but we have to be careful."

They had six sleigh dogs, but Wolfy was John's favourite. He was a playful mongrel. When the boy and his father came out of the cabin the shaggy gray dog knew he was coming along. He jumped and pulled on his chain, wagged his fluffy tail and barked with joy.

Soon they were on their way. The old man held onto the leash on the dog. The dog was in the harness, pulling a small sleigh on which the boy sat. There was a broad smile on John's face. Sure enough, the ice was good and solid all the way along the shore. Way out on the middle of the lake there was still water where it was not yet frozen.

There were some fresh tracks near the shore about two miles from the cabin. John's father went to have a closer look at them. Suddenly Wolfy let out a loud bark and jumped forward, pulling the leash out of the man's hand. He started running towards the middle of the lake. With the sudden movement, John's hands locked around the chain that held down the head of the sleigh.

"Whoa, Wolfy," John cried, the cold wind blowing in his face.

John's father began to chase them. "Whoa Wolfy, whoa Wolfy," he called.

Some places made the dog slip and slide, but on he ran, his tail wagging, the sleigh swinging back and forth.

"Whoa, Wolfy," his father's voice was getting farther away, the open water on the lake was coming closer. Still the dog ran on.

The man slipped and fell and the ice began to crack. He could not move. He knew if he did move his weight would break the ice. Far out on the lake he could hear the dog barking, heading straight for the open water.

"Oh no," he said. He could not bear to look.

The ice was beginning to crack alongside the sleigh now. John was terrified, yet held on.

Out of nowhere a huge bird appeared in front of the dog. Wolfy began to chase it. With its widespread wings, the eagle made a circle back toward the shore, toward where the man lay on the soft ice.

As the eagle, the dog, and the boy on the sleigh passed by him, a feather dropped not far from the man. He reached for it, and curled his finger around the feather. When he moved, the ice did not crack. Cautiously, he got on his hands and knees. Then he slowly crawled until he was sure the ice was solid under him. Then he ran to where the dog rested near the shore, with the boy. He hugged his son.

"Thank God, you're all right," he said. Wolfy was sitting on the ice beside the sleigh, his tongue hanging out.

"Thank the eagle," John said. With the feather still in his hand, the old man looked up. The great bird made a circle and glided into the clouds.

Tale of the Stone

Harvey Knight

What Lindsay loved most about summer was the Saturday afternoon trips with her parents to the countryside. It was a time for Mom and Dad to fish and relax in the sunshine and for Lindsay to explore. She loved being outside. Every Saturday she would discover something new in nature. Lindsay was filled with wonder at everything she saw, from the tiniest bug in the grass to the giant shapes of clouds in the sky.

This afternoon in the country, though, was different. Mom and Dad decided to fish along a river that had a stony shore. Lindsay decided that today was just right for picking stones.

There were so many stones on that shore, big and small, flat and round. Some were grey, others brown. While Mom and Dad fished, Lindsay carefully collected a handful of little stones. Out of this handful she chose one that was especially pretty. It was grey, round and smooth, with sparkly specks all over it.

"Oh Dad, look at the pretty stone I found," Lindsay said, as she held it up close to Dad's face.

5

Dad, who also loved nature, thought this was a perfect time to tell Lindsay a story about stones.

"Stones are very special," he began. "They have been around for a long, long time. They were here even before people lived on this earth. Stones have knowledge and wisdom," Dad continued, "because they have been taken on countless journeys throughout the history of the world. That's why stones, like the one you have in your hand, are so round and smooth. They get that way from rolling down hillsides, or being taken by streams and rivers..."

As Dad began his story, Lindsay took the stone and brought it close to her face, peering so closely at it that it made her cross-eyed.

"Hi Lindsay, can you rub that chunk of dirt off me?"

"Oh sure. Right here...Hey, you're talking to me," Lindsay said in astonishment.

"Of course I'm talking to you. I've been lying around for so many years with no one to talk to. I'm bored and I'm lonesome, sure glad you came along."

"Have you lived here all your life?" Lindsay asked, as she rubbed the dirt off the smooth surface of the stone.

"Yeah, as a matter of fact, I've lived in this particular place for a few thousand years. Would you like me to tell you of the places I've lived?" Lindsay nodded her head. "Well, I have lived in the water and felt the wet lips of fish nibbling at bugs and other tiny creatures who made their home on me. Living in the water was good for me by the way. I had a bath every day.

"But I've had more exciting times than just being nibbled at while I lived in the river. Sometimes great floods came and strong water currents took me down the river to far-off places. Those underwater journeys were fun, moving to new homes, having new stones for neighbours and being nibbled at by strange new fish.

"On dry land, I've felt the light footsteps of mice and weasels as they scampered over me. Sometimes more considerate animals look-ing for a meal of bugs, would turn me over. Ah, this was a great treat for it would give my belly a chance to feel the warmth of the sun and a fresh breeze.

"Sometimes I would feel the cold wet nose of a large animal such as a buffalo, as he ate the grass around me. I always thanked them for cutting my lawn so I could see more countryside and sky. Often these large animals would accidentally kick me and send me rolling down hillsides, or I'd end up in their stomachs and go for strange, dark journeys with rumbling adventures.

"In other times, I've met creatures you've never seen, 'cause it was so long ago. It was before people lived on this earth. Some were giant cold-blooded creatures with claws as long as a man's leg. Whenever they stepped on me, it hurt so much I felt like cracking. I sometimes went on trips in their stomachs, too.

"But the long, slow journeys were the best, although these didn't happen too often. When the ice ages came, they'd push me slowly over great distances. These were the trips with plenty of excitement and adventure. With every ice age, I get to see a lot of places and meet other stones and creatures, some friendly, some not so friend-ly. I'm looking forward to the next one coming along.

"Not so long ago, right here on this shore, some very tall people stopped by for awhile. We had a lot in common, those tall people and I, for we could spend years at a stretch telling each other stories about our travels through the ages. They lived thousands of years and travelled far and wide, you know. So they knew almost as much as I did about the land and everything that lived on it, or in it. A human couldn't live long enough to listen to one of their stories because it would sometimes take five hundred years to get to the point. Yes, storytelling was an important tradition for the tall people. They wouldn't dare make a long story short. And they didn't like it very much if you tried to interrupt them while they told their tale.

"There were others I often met called little people. These people were no taller than a rabbit standing on its hind legs. These people would sometimes come along and pick me up and take me to their homes, which were built inside river banks. There they would give me royal treatment. As long as I told them some interesting things, they would repay me by bathing me in the finest perfumes made from plants. They would sometimes wrap me in finely woven silver cloth and take me on their adventures through tall dark forests and over rolling hills. After many adventures they would bring me back to the very same spot where they found me. It was wonderful to travel with such an enchanting people."

Stone was quiet for a moment, then as if remembering something he jumped and Lindsay almost dropped him.

"My goodness, it's getting late," he said. "It's almost time for you to go home. I do get carried away. I really like you, Lindsay. Hey, why don't you take me home for awhile? Perhaps we could share some more stories. I would really like to know more about your world."

"Oh, I would like that," Lindsay replied. "There are so many things you could teach me. Do you think I could keep you forever?"

"Not forever, Lindsay, because we both have our own journeys. One day you must bring me back to this place so that I can continue mine and you can go on yours."

"I promise to bring you back," Lindsay said, rubbing the stone gently and putting it carefully into her sweater pocket.

"Time to go home, Lindsay," Dad called, putting the fishing gear into the car. "Did you have a good time this afternoon?"

"Yes Dad, it was a wonderful day," Lindsay said, climbing into the car. As they drove back to the city, Lindsay thought that this was the best afternoon she had ever had in her entire life.

The Pillars of Paclian

Jordan Wheeler

Chuck stepped on a worm. He lifted his runner and saw the flattened remains. It didn't bother him. After all, it was just a worm, and now a dead worm.

He was angry. Not at the worm, nor the dog he had yelled at, the cat he'd chased, the garbage can he'd kicked over, or the stop sign he'd thrown a rock at. He was mad at his mother for making him clean the yard and at his little brother for not helping him. He got so mad thinking about it, he wandered off without doing it. Down the backlane he marched until he came to the riverbank.

Now he was sitting up in a tree. He flicked an ant off the branch he was sitting on and watched it sail to the ground, then walk away.

"Why can't I do that?" he said and grew angrier.

Chuck sat back and closed his eyes. But something strange began to happen. Even though his eyes were closed, he could still see everything around him. He opened his eyes and saw the same sights. A railroad bridge to his right and above, the leaves shimmering in the wind overhead, the dusty ground and shrubs. He felt a very disquieting effect begin to take place.

He stared with closed eyes at the bridge. Suddenly it changed from black to green, then it was flooded with yellow, intermingled with waves of red as its shape expanded in size. It seemed to move from above him down below him and to his left.

The leaves in the tree turned a penetrating colour he had never seen before, and into a shape he had never experienced. One that reached out to him while moving away and so remained motionless but tingling with vibrant, whispering glitters of light. They were alive, a tingling mass that shuddered and filtered into the sky, changing all colour, all light, all shapes.

Nothing stayed in its place anymore. He fell up from his tree through the bridge below and swirled about in the sky. There was no direction, no distance. All he could see was changing colours and changing shapes. A streak of indigo flashed through his legs, a lethargic body of maroon funneled into nothing and re-emerged as blue swirling into violet.

He was carried along by a force he didn't recognize. He was scared. Nothing seemed real, but there it was. He had never seen anything like this. The sounds were notes that absorbed each other or spread apart at random in an orchestrated chaos of whistles, whispers and whines. He had never heard anything like this. In growing terror, he opened his eyes.

He was standing on solid ground. He felt relieved, yet quite puzzled. His tree was gone, and so was the river and the railroad bridge. Around him stood very large, very tall blades of grass. Most towered over his head and were nearly as wide as he was. He touched the edges of the blades and felt their incredible sharpness. He would have to be careful walking about lest he cut himself on these blades.

Wondering where he was and what he was doing here, he sat down on a large boulder between two blades of grass. He was muddled and confused.

"It's about time you got here," called a voice ahead of him.

"Who's there?" Chuck called.

"Don't worry, it's just me," and through the tall blades of grass slithered a long reddish-pink earthworm. Its body was as wide as Chuck's leg, but much longer. "You look scared. Didn't you know you were coming here?"

"No," Chuck squealed.

"Don't be scared, you're too big for me to eat. I guess I forgot part of the procedure, we haven't done this for a while, you know."

"Done what?"

"This, the 'respect for anthropoids program.' You were supposed to be briefed on what to expect. My fault! Do you have any questions?"

"Yeah!"

"Shoot!"

Chuck shot rapidly, "Who are you? Where am I? What am I doing here?"

"Hold it! One at a time. My name is Sleodanpilpiyane but my friends call me Sloon. You are among the Pillars of Paclian."

"Where?"

"The Pillars of Paclian."

"Never heard of it," muttered Chuck, finding all this a little hard to believe.

"The Pillars are the blades of grass around us. We call them pillars because in our legends, they were created to hold up the sky so we could move about safely underneath. Paclian is the name of the area.

You know it as your back lawn."

This didn't surprise Chuck. By now he was ready for anything.

"So why am I here?"

"Don't you know?" asked Sloon.

"No!"

"Geez, I guess we really messed up. Okay, I'll tell you. Remember earlier today when you walked from your house to the river?"

"Yes," said Chuck hesitantly.

"Well, as you were walking along, you stepped on one of us. On purpose, if I recall."

Chuck realized he had been brought here to be punished for stepping on that other worm. He suddenly grew frantically apologetic. "I'm sorry, I didn't mean it. Don't hurt me. I'll do anything you want but don't hurt me."

"Settle down, I'm not going to hurt you."

"You're not mad?"

"Not really. You stepped on my brother, Biwoobit, but I guess he deserved it. Everyone knows slithering around sidewalks is dangerous. Through the years, we have come to accept being stepped on, so when it happens we don't get too upset. But when it's done on purpose, we wonder why. In the old days, we used to bring humans here quite often so we could ask them. That was back when we were always being hung on fish hooks. But now humans are using other kinds of bait, we've let it slide. Recently though, we've felt a need to ask because we're being stepped on more often, but we seem to have forgotten exactly how to go about asking. We sent a message by mosquito to the tree you were in. The mosquito relayed the message to an ant who was supposed to prepare you for all this. I guess somehow he never reached you."

Chuck remembered the ant on the branch.

"So," continued Sloon, "why did you step on Biwoobit?"

"I was mad."

"Is that all?" shouted Sloon. "You were mad, so you stepped on my brother?"

"Well, yeah. I guess so."

"Did you ever think how that might feel to Biwoobit?"

"No."

"That's the trouble with you humans, you care only about yourselves. Why were you mad?"

"My mother told me to clean up the backyard and my little brother wouldn't help me."

"And that's why you squished Biwoobit? Why didn't you squish your brother instead?" asked Sloon.

"It was easier to squish Biwoobit."

"Oh, I see," said Sloon. "Let me ask you a question. What are you?"

"Metis."

"That's not what I meant."

"Male?" asked Chuck.

"No, I mean yes, but what else?"

"Hungry."

"Keep going."

"Five-foot-five, smart, goaltender, eleven."

"How do you feel when someone bigger and older than you picks on you?"

"Mad."

"So how do you think we feel when someone steps on us?" Sloon asked.

Before Chuck could answer, the ground began to shake and tremble violently.

"What's that?" Chuck asked, alarmed.

"I think that's your brother walking this way. Don't forget, you're the size of a beetle right now."

The trembling got worse. Chuck could see a gigantic figure approaching from the east, casting a cold shadow over them. They watched a large foot fill the sky and descend upon them.

"Quick, close your eyes," urged Sloon.

Chuck obeyed, but still saw the foot coming. He could make out the tread design and the company logo of his brother's sneaker. Down came the foot, landing on top of Chuck, passing through him, then spraying into a million colours.

"That was close," said Sloon.

Once again Chuck found himself floating among sounds, colours, and shapes.

"How do you feel?" Sloon asked.

"Where are you?"

"Right here," answered Sloon.

"Where am I?"

"Wherever you are, I suppose. We are in a state of change. Right now we could become anything, anywhere. But we must be careful not to become nothing, nowhere, or everything, everywhere. There is a big difference. We are anything, the colours and shapes you see are nothing, and what we feel is everything. Do you understand?"

"No."

"Being anything, we see nothing, but feel everything. Open your eyes."

Chuck opened his eyes.

The colours, shapes and sounds had disappeared and there was a bright light shining into his eyes.

"What do you see?" asked Sloon.

"I see large teeth beside me, a huge tongue above me. I feel rotten and wet, and I can't move."

"That's right, and if you wait a second you'll see why."

"Where are you?"

"I am a set of pliers in a dentist's hand. You are a rotten tooth about to be pulled out. Get ready, here I come."

And Sloon entered the mouth and pulled Chuck out. They closed their eyes and re-entered the sea of colours.

"How do you feel?" asked Sloon.

"Sad."

"Why?"

"If I had been taken care of, you wouldn't have had to pull me out."

"Do you feel that way about your teeth?"

"No, they're just teeth."

"But now you know how a tooth feels."

"Yeah! I never knew a tooth could feel. I guess I should take better care of them."

"Now you're beginning to understand. This might not take as long as I thought. Open your eyes again."

Chuck opened his eyes. He couldn't understand what he saw, and he felt himself spinning around and around.

"How do you feel?" Sloon asked.

"Strange, sort of electrical."

"That's not strange. You are an electron of a hydrogen atom. I am the neutron at the centre and you are spinning around me. We are joined to an oxygen atom and there is another hydrogen atom on the other side. All three of us make up a water molecule."

"Where are we?" asked Chuck.

"We are on top of a kitchen counter in an electric kettle. We're going to be coffee in a few minutes."

"I feel very small."

"Don't worry, you are. But you are also one of millions of equally important electrons that will eventually be drunk from a cup. You have a purpose."

"It's fun spinning around like this."

"Yeah, and it would be interesting to stay here and see where we would end up. But you're making me dizzy, so close your eyes," and they re-entered the sea of colours.

"Now what am I going to be?" Chuck asked.

"I don't know."

"You don't?"

"I have a general idea, but nothing is ever certain. Never depend on what might happen. Open your eyes."

Chuck opened his eyes. Around him was the night sky. Wherever he looked, all he could see were stars pitted against blackness. Within himself, he felt tremendous heat and great power.

"Wow! I've never seen this before," Sloon said. "Billions of humans are depending on you. Some of them are even worshipping you. The earth itself is dependent on you. I am a flame on your surface and you are the sun."

"Where is earth?"

"It's too small, you can't see it. To you the earth isn't important. You know it is there, but you don't really care. You don't need it."

Chuck had never felt that way about the earth before.

"I don't like being the sun," he said.

"Why not? You are the most powerful and most important object in this solar system."

"I feel alone."

Sloon let him feel like that for a little while.

"Good," he said at last, "close your eyes."

Back in the sea of colours, Chuck didn't speak. He just floated along thinking of the sun, the earth, and himself.

"Do you understand why I took you here?" asked Sloon.

"Yeah, I think so."

"That's good, I had faith in you. Let's go back now. Open your eyes."

Chuck found himself back among the Pillars of Paclian with Sloon slithering close by.

"No place like home," Sloon marvelled. "So how do you feel after all that?"

"I never knew my whole planet could seem small and unimportant."

"Smaller than Biwoobit, eh? Now you know how it feels to be as small as Biwoobit. No matter how large, and powerful, or how small anything is, it has a place in this universe. It has a right to exist. You have that right, I have that right, and Biwoobit had that right, and nothing should interfere with that right. No matter how small or unimportant something seems, its right to exist must be respected."

"Yeah. You have to respect everything," announced Chuck.

"Good. You have learned all you were supposed to by coming here. It is time for you to go back."

"Will I ever see you again?"

"I slither around a lot. If you see a worm, it might be me."

"Can I ever go on these journeys again?"

"Sure, just close your eyes and let your imagination carry you. You can go anywhere you want. Become anything anywhere."

"Promise?"

"Yeah. And who knows, maybe some day I'll go with you."

"I'd like that," Chuck said. He took one last, long look at Sleodan-pilpiyane, then closed his eyes.

Chuck cleaned the yard and did his other chores around the house more often in the days to follow. Never again did he purposely step on a worm and he tried not to hurt anyone else. He often thought of Sloon and when he really missed the worm, he would close his eyes and once more probe the Pillars of Paclian.

18   *Dress for Ara,* Ruth Cuthand

She Chose to Dance Instead of Putting Peas in Her Shoes, Ruth Cuthand 19

Ruth Cuthand

"I was born in 1954 in Prince Albert, Saskatchewan. I received my BFA degree from the University of Saskatchewan in 1983.

"My world view is from the perspective of the Plains Cree culture, therefore I do not accept the latest phrase being used by non-Indians: 'the blending of cultures.' I believe that this phrase is a misnomer and does not respect the culturally different artist. There is a definite distinction between culture and technology."

about **Dress for Ara** and **She Chose to Dance Instead of Putting Peas in Her Shoes**:

"Since 1983, I have been working on a series of paintings with the shirt/dress as the main image. This imagery is based on the original clothing worn by the participants of the Ghost Dance Religion. This clothing was painted with the participants' personal symbols and was worn to celebrate and protect that person.

"The shirts/dresses that I create are not meant to be worn by physical beings, but are rather for the spirit of that being, whether animate or inanimate.

"The shirt/dress is always in isolation and directs itself to the viewer. This forces the viewer to enter into a dialogue with the work, instead of being a voyeur. The viewer is then in a position to take as much or as little as he can from the work."

Gerald McMaster

Gerald McMaster was born in 1953 in North Battleford, Saskatchewan. From 1973-75 he attended the Institute of American Indian Art in Sante Fe, New Mexico, and from 1975-77 the Minneapolis College of Art and Design, from which he received his BFA.

Gerald was the art co-ordinator for the Indian Federated College in Regina from 1977-81. Since then has been curator of contemporary Indian Art at the National Museum of Man in Ottawa.

about **When Legends Die**:

"One weekend a friend was showing me some tricks with watercolour and this began as an exercise. But I had the idea of the Indian, with his headdress and horse, riding the prairie. People have romanticized this individual, this race, made a legend, a myth out of it. They have tried to return to that time, live that legend. But that myth is dead. You cannot return. You can continue certain traditions, but you have to live in the realities of today."

about **Mystical Protection**:

"At one time, the shield provided protection—from arrows. But it couldn't protect you from guns, so it became a symbolic object. Instead of physical protection, then it gave psychological strength or "mystical protection." That's why I made it hazy."

22   *Mystical Protection*, Gerald McMaster

When Legends Die, Gerald McMaster 23

Ray Keighley

"I am half Cree and have always been interested in Indian art. When I was living on the West Coast I visited coastal Indian museums containing totem poles and carving. Out of those visits came a desire to construct an animal of my own design.

"The **Mystic Moose** print came as a result of doodling and having fun on a small piece of paper. It looked so interesting I decided to make it into a large silkscreen print.

"I have always been interested in the imaginative or ideal world and how it coincides with reality. That is why the moose form and the landscape resemble reality but the elements that make them up are stylized.

"When I was younger I had an instructor who told me I should capture the spirit of the animal and this is as close as I have come to doing that, so I called the print 'Mystic Moose.'"

Edward Poitras

"In my work I try to express a world view through use of material and image. My cultural reality and heritage are combined and assimilated into one object of expression.

"This assimilation is a fact of cultural development. As artists I feel we are responsible for our own cultural development and expression. We have the freedom to express ourselves culturally and to make ourselves understood as a unique group of people."

about **As Snow Before the Summer Sun**:

"In my sculpture, **As Snow Before the Summer Sun**, I tried to express the negative aspect of assimilation, where one culture dominates another and forces assimilation, through the replacement of image and material. This is a warning and a compromise with the understanding of what was."

26   *Mystic Moose*, Ray Keighley

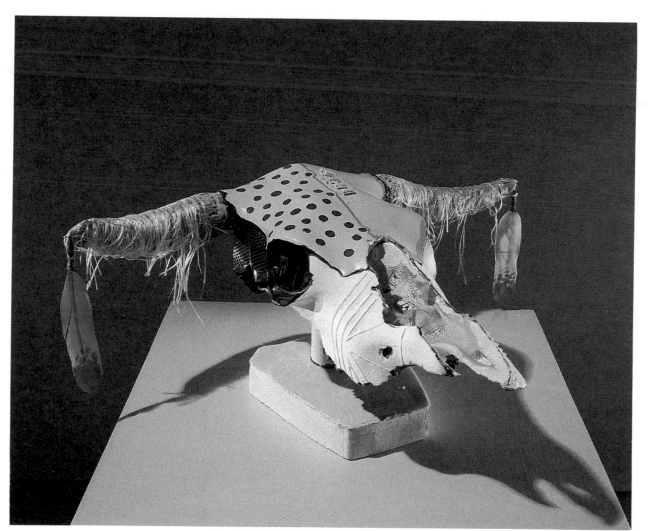

As Snow Before the Summer Sun, Edward Poitras 27

Bob Boyer

Bob Boyer was born in 1948 in Prince Albert, Saskatchewan. He received his B.Ed. (in Art Education) from the University of Saskatchewan, Regina Campus, in 1971.

From 1971-73 Bob taught art and drama in Prince Albert. Since 1973 he has been in Regina, at the Norman Mackenzie Gallery and then the Saskatchewan Indian Federated College, University of Regina. Since 1980 he has been head of the Department of Indian Art at the College.

*about **How Cola**:*

*"**How Cola** was part of a series of drawings and watercolours in which I was playing with abstract elements of Indian shields.*

"I usually put puns—visual and verbal—in my work. In this one it was a play on the Pepsi and Coca Cola shields that used to be on stores. When Sioux talk to each other, the word they use to mean friend or brother is 'cola' and 'how' means hello."

Raymond McCallum

Raymond McCallum is from the Flying Dust Band near Meadow Lake and now lives on the Sakimay Reservation.

During 1972-73 Ray studied art with Sarain Stump. From 1973-75 he worked in the Graphic Arts Department at the Saskatchewan Indian Cultural College in Saskatoon and from 1975-79 was the illustrator for the curriculum studies and research department at the College.

From 1979-82 he added accounting to his skills, through a training-on-the-job program. Since then he has done accounting for the College and has worked as a freelance artist in Regina.

The three pieces selected for this book were also featured in the 1984 Saskatchewan Indian Cultural College calendar.

about **Frost Moon**:

"The Dene people of northern Saskatchewan have always had a special relationship to the land, depending on it for their livelihood. Many changes, however, have taken place since they have had better access to modern conveniences. The differences and the breaking of this interdependence is shown in **Frost Moon**. The walls of the house and modern clothing represent the non-traditional Dene lifestyle which has set the Dene apart from their traditional roots, represented by the coyote."

30   *How Cola,* Bob Boyer

Frost Moon, Raymond McCallum

31

Play With Me

Jordan Wheeler

"Momma, why do I have to go to school?" asked Tod as his mother braided his long hair.

"You have to learn," she answered.

"But I don't like school," he pouted.

"Why not?"

"None of the other kids play with me, and they all ride their bikes and I don't have one."

"Well Tod, having a bike isn't everything, you know."

"I wish you wouldn't always say you can't afford one. Maybe if Dad comes back he'll buy one."

"Your father isn't going to come back, Tod."

"Why not?"

"I've told you many times already. Your father did something bad and he has to go away for a long time."

"Jail, huh?"

"Yes," she said.

"A lot of other kids have fathers. Maybe that's why they have bikes, too."

"I don't think so. There," she said.

Tod's mother had finished braiding his hair. He put on his jacket and opened the front door.

"See you later, Tod," said his mother.

"Bye, mom," he answered.

He walked down the steps and on to the sidewalk under the bright morning sun. It usually took him fifteen minutes to walk to school, but only five if he ran. He was a bit late, so he started running. He ran as fast as his running shoes could take him. His running shoes had holes on the sides. They had belonged to his cousin before they were given to him. So had his blue jeans, which were patched at the knees.

Tod's mom didn't have a lot of money. She worked hard at a factory while Tod was at school. For as long as he could remember, she had worked. Even when his dad was at home. Tod couldn't remember if his dad worked. He was only three when his father went away with the police. Now he was six and in grade one at school.

At first, Tod liked going to school because it was new and exciting. But after awhile, he didn't like it because the other kids wouldn't play with him. So Tod was almost always alone. He thought if he had a bicycle like everyone else, he wouldn't be alone. But he knew his mother couldn't afford one.

Sometimes Tod thought the others at school were better than him because they could afford things like bicycles. His mother always told him he should be proud because he was Indian. But sometimes he didn't feel proud, just different. When he got to the school fence, he stopped running and tried to catch his breath. A boy rode by on his bicycle and Tod recognized him.

"Hi, Dean!" he yelled.

"Hi, Tod," Dean called over his shoulder, but he kept on riding his bike.

Tod walked slowly into school and went to his classroom. Everyone was talking, but Tod couldn't find anyone to talk to. He sat down at his desk and waited.

Finally Tod's teacher, Miss Boorhammer, entered the classroom. She told everyone to stand up for the Lord's Prayer and "O Canada." Tod felt somewhat embarrassed because after seven weeks of school, he still didn't know the Lord's Prayer or "O Canada." But he moved his lips and pretended so no one would notice.

After "O Canada," Miss Boorhammer told the class to take out their math books. Tod was glad. He was good in math.

The math lesson went on for the first half of the morning. Miss Boorhammer asked many of the children questions and none of them knew the answers. Tod wished she would ask him a question because he knew the answers. He always put up his hand, but she never called on him. This made Tod mad.

Finally, just before recess, Miss Boorhammer looked at Tod and said, "Tod, can you tell the class what nine plus seven makes?"

Tod thought quickly. The question was a hard one.

"Sixteen," he said at last.

"That's correct. Good, Tod. How many of the rest of you had the right answer?"

Nearly everyone put up their hands, but Tod knew they were lying. He didn't care. He had it right and that was all that mattered. He felt better.

Maybe the others would play with him now because he had the right answer, he thought. But when they all went out at recess to play baseball, no one asked Tod to play.

"That's okay," he said to himself. "I don't like baseball anyway." But he knew that wasn't true. He just didn't know how to play baseball, and he was too shy to ask the others to teach him. He thought they would make fun of him. So he sat on the ground.

He watched a colony of ants building their nest and gathering food. One ant was trying to carry a Smarty back to the nest. The Smarty was large. Tod thought if the ant can't carry it, how is it going to eat it? Another ant came along, but even two of them couldn't carry the Smarty. More and more ants arrived and it finally took six of the little red ants to move the Smarty back to the nest. But when they got there, they found out the Smarty was too big to get into the hole. A whole pile of ants started breaking the Smarty into pieces while other ants made the hole larger. After several minutes, the ants finally got the last bits of the Smarty down into their home. Tod thought the ants were smart to be able to do such a thing.

The buzzer went off, meaning recess was over. Tod looked up and saw kids running toward him on their way back to class. He was worried they might step on the ant's nest so he put his right knee on one side of the hole, and his left foot on the other. Then he pretended he was tying his shoelace until everyone went by. When he was sure the ants were safe, he got up and hurried back into school.

Lunch time finally came and Tod started his walk home. He watched as Dean and the others got on their bicycles and peddled away.

When he arrived at home, he walked slowly up the wooden stairs and checked to see if there was any mail. Tod's mother always told him to bring in the mail and leave it on the kitchen table for her.

After leaving the letters on the table, he washed his hands and made his lunch: a bologna sandwich with lettuce, an apple, and a glass of milk. His mother had taught him how to make his own lunch because she couldn't be home to make it for him. When he finished eating, it was time to go back to school. He cleaned up his mess, put on his jacket, and left the house, making sure the door was locked.

The boys in his class were playing baseball when he walked into the schoolyard.

"Hey Tod, we need a third baseman," shouted Scott, a friend of Dean. "Do you want to play?"

"Sure," yelled Tod. At last he was going to get to play. But he stopped suddenly before reaching the playing field. He remembered he didn't know how to play baseball.

"What's the matter?" asked Scott.

"Nothing," said Tod. He didn't want them to make fun of him, so he didn't say a thing. He borrowed Dean's glove and went to third base. At least he knew where it was.

They played for about ten minutes and Tod was feeling very lucky, even though his team was losing. He wasn't worried about winning, he just didn't want anyone to hit the ball at him. So far, no one had. Then Dean came up at bat. The first pitch was too low, but Dean hit the second pitch with a loud smack and it flew over Tod and into left field. Tod watched the left fielder, Hank, run after the ball. It took him a long time to get out and pick it up. Then he threw it. Tod swallowed hard. Hank had thrown it straight at him. It was a mighty throw and Tod watched it sail higher and higher into the air. When it started falling, Tod held up his glove and aimed it at the ball. Closer and closer the ball came and at last it landed in the glove. He squeezed as hard as he could so the ball wouldn't fall out, and then he smiled. He had caught his first baseball. But when he turned around, he suddenly saw Dean running straight at him. He was so startled, he jumped out of his way as Dean slid into the base.

"What did you do that for, Tod?" yelled Hank.

"Do what?" asked Tod.

"You dummy. You were supposed to tag him," Scott shouted at him. Just then the buzzer went off and everyone went inside.

"We won't even get last bats because of you, Tod," said Hank, walking past him. Tod felt terrible. He dropped the glove and ran out of the schoolyard and down the street as fast as he could, tears falling from his eyes. When he couldn't run any further, he stopped and sat on the curb. Now they will never play with me, he thought.

"I wish I was like them," he said to himself, looking at the braids hanging down the front of his jacket. "I wish I had a bicycle and could play baseball. I wish I had blonde hair and I wish I had a father who could afford to buy me things."

Tod was about to start crying again, when he heard another cry. He listened and it came again. It was a meow. Tod finally spotted the kitten way up in a tree in front of a large house. He walked over to the tree and looked up at the kitten.

"What's the matter?" asked Tod.

"Meow," said the kitten.

"You're stuck up there, aren't you?"

"Meow," said the kitten.

"And you want to come down, don't you?"

"Meow," said the kitten, a little louder.

"But how can I get you down?" asked Tod.

The kitten was silent.

Tod thought for a few minutes and then decided to phone the fire department. No one was home at the house, so he went to the gas station at the corner and asked if he could use their phone. Then he went back to the kitten.

"A firefighter is going to come and get you down, little kitten."

"Meow," said the kitten, as if to say thank you.

Tod watched the big yellow fire truck come down the street. There were hoses, ladders and compartments for equipment all over the truck, and the wheels were taller than Tod. He thought of how exciting it must be for a firefighter to drive that huge truck around and put out fires. The truck stopped in front of Tod and two firefighters got out.

"Hi there. Are you the boy who phoned us?" asked the first firefighter.

"Yeah," answered Tod. "The kitten is stuck up there in the tree."

"Meow," said the kitten.

"Okay, we'll get you down from there," said the second firefighter. Tod noticed the second had dark skin like his own.

"Meow," said the kitten.

Both firefighters took a ladder off the side of the truck and put it up against the tree.

"Do you want to help me?" the dark-skinned one asked Tod.

"Sure," said Tod.

"Hold the ladder while I climb up the tree, all right?"

"Okay."

"Meow," said the kitten.

The firefighter climbed almost to the top of the ladder. He picked the kitten off a branch up high in the tree and brought it down, holding it with one hand against his yellow coat. He gave the kitten to Tod.

"Thanks," said Tod.

"Purrr," said the kitten.

"How old is she?" asked the firefighter.

"I don't know. She doesn't live with me."

"You mean you saved the life of a kitten you don't even know?"

"Yeah."

"What's your name?"

"Tod."

"Glad to meet a hero like you, Tod. My name is Wayne," and they shook hands. Tod felt very proud and happy. He had never been called a hero before.

"Boy, do I get a reward?" asked Tod.

"Well, knowing they've saved a life is a reward in itself for most heroes," Wayne told him.

Tod put the kitten on the ground and watched it run up to the house and lie down on the steps. He felt satisfied knowing it was safe.

"I guess you're right. But I was hoping for a bike."

"Why would you want a bike?"

"To be like the other kids at school so they will play with me."

"Aren't you like them now?"

"No, I'm different from them, I'm Indian. If I had a bike I would be a little like them, and then maybe they wouldn't leave me out all the time."

Wayne looked at Tod for a moment. "Tod," he said at last, "are you proud you're Indian?"

"Well, yeah, but sometimes I wish I wasn't so I could be like other kids."

Wayne thought for a minute. "Listen, Tod. I don't have to work this afternoon. Why don't we phone your parents and ask if you can spend some time with me. How does that sound?"

"Sure," said Tod and the two of them walked to the gas station and phoned Tod's mother. Wayne did most of the talking and after Tod's mother agreed, they walked back to the fire truck. The door was too high for Tod; Wayne had to lift him up and help him in.

Tod felt very important, riding in a huge fire truck between two firefighters. He imagined them on their way to a fire, speeding through the streets with red lights flashing and the siren blaring away. Then rushing to the fire hydrant with the hose and spraying the flame with water.

At the station, Tod watched Wayne get ready to leave. He took off his rubber overalls and rubber boots. When he took off his helmet, Tod saw his long, black hair fall down past his shoulders. Wayne slid a button beside his name on a board on the wall to show he was leaving for the day. He said good-bye to the other firefighters who were playing cards, waiting for emergencies. Wayne and Tod walked to Wayne's car.

"How long have you been a firefighter?" asked Tod.

"Eleven years."

"Boy. I didn't know Indians could be firefighters."

"Indians can be whatever they want, just like anyone else. I have a friend who is a teacher, and my younger sister is going to be a veterinarian."

"A what?"

"A veterinarian. A doctor for animals."

"Boy, does that mean I can be a firefighter like you?"

"Sure, when you're older. But it takes hard work."

"I'll work hard," thought Tod as they drove to Wayne's apartment.

Tod was surprised when Wayne unlocked the door and led Tod into his apartment. There were paintings on the wall like the one his mother had brought home a few months before. They had long, curving black lines coming from animals. His mother's painting had been an eagle. Wayne had one of an eagle too, but there were others as well. One was a painting of an old man with long white hair and many wrinkles on his face. It reminded him of his grandfather.

"Want a glass of orange juice?" asked Wayne.

"Sure," said Tod.

Wayne went into the kitchen and Tod sat in the living room. On a shelf beside some books, there was some braided sweetgrass. When Wayne came back with the orange juice, Tod asked what it was for.

"I burn a little bit of it when I pray," Wayne told him.

"My mother has some, too. She burns it all the time."

"You should ask her about it and maybe you could help her pray."

"Did you have a father when you were a boy?" asked Tod.

"Yeah. But I didn't see him very often. When I was your age, I was sent to a city to stay with a family and I only got to go home for summer."

"Why?"

"I had to go to school and where I grew up, there wasn't one."

"Did you like school?"

"Not at first. It was hard and the other kids would ignore me or make fun of me because I had long hair and I was dark. But after awhile, they quit making fun of me."

"Why did they quit?"

"I guess they found out I wasn't much different from them after all, besides my colour. Some of them still made fun of me, but not as many and not as often. I made enough friends so it didn't bother me."

"Didn't you want to be like them?"

"For a long time I wished I wasn't Indian. But I remembered my mother telling me I would always be Indian, and that I should be proud. I tried, but it was hard to be proud. Then when I started making friends, they would ask me about Indians and I told them as much as I knew. That's the first time I was proud to be Indian."

"I hope I can make friends at school."

"You will. But wanting to be like them won't help."

For the rest of the afternoon, Tod listened to Wayne tell stories

41

about rescuing people and putting out fires. Tod listened very intently because he had decided that someday he was going to be a firefighter.

It was almost supper time when Wayne drove Tod home. Just as they pulled up in front of Tod's house, Dean and Scott rode past on their bicycles. When they saw Tod, they stopped.

"Hey Tod, how come you weren't at school this afternoon? Everyone was wondering where you were," said Scott.

"Tod did some work for the fire department this afternoon," Wayne said as Tod got out of the car.

"Wow," said Dean.

"Tod's a real hero," Wayne added.

"You want to play baseball at the school?" Scott asked Tod. "We're having a big game."

Tod thought hard for a moment. He hadn't seen his mother, who was standing in the doorway of their house.

"I don't know," he said. "I might have to eat supper right now."

"It's okay, Tod," his mother said. "Supper won't be ready for another hour. Go ahead with your friends and play baseball."

For a moment, Tod remained on the sidewalk. Then he broke into the biggest smile that had ever come across his face.

"Okay!" he yelled. "Let's go!"

As Tod ran alongside Scott and Dean, who were still on their bicycles, towards the school, Wayne got out of the car.

"Thank you so much," Tod's mother said. "I haven't seen him so happy in years."

"That's okay," Wayne said. "He reminds me a lot of me when I was his age. He's a fine boy."

Tod's mother smiled. "Do you want to come in for a cup of coffee?" she asked.

42

"Sure," Wayne said, and they went into the house.

The Hockey Game

Wes Fineday

The knocking at my door woke me up. It was a Saturday morning, which meant that there was no school. I got out of bed, got
dressed, then walked out of my bedroom and across the hallway
to the bathroom. The door was closed. Someone was in there. I went
back to the bedroom, made my bed, picked up my books and put
them on the dresser. I had been doing my homework just before
I fell asleep. There was still quite a bit to do.

Grade nine sure wasn't easy, at least not as easy as grade eight.
I had finished my grade eight at boarding school last year, had done
quite well in fact. This year was different. The Department of Indian
Affairs had sent me to live in Moose Jaw to do my grade nine. They
had explained to me that they had found me a "good Christian boarding home" to live in. They also told me I should consider myself
lucky to have this opportunity. At the time I wondered if it would
be anything like the school I had left.

I went back to the bathroom. It was vacant. I had a good wash and went back to the bedroom.

They had driven me to Moose Jaw from the boarding school and with that move everything had changed. Now I was in a bedroom by myself instead of a dormitory with thirty other kids. The food eaten by these Christians was unlike anything I ever got at boarding school or at home. For breakfast they would eat dry cereal and pour milk over it to make it soggy. With this they ate toast that was also soggy with butter. For lunch and supper we would have meat and potatoes or rice. I'd eaten these before but not the way this woman cooked it. She used tomatoes and stuff that looked like powder that she kept in small jars over the stove. She must have had twenty different kinds of powder. It was awful. My stomach would hurt for hours after and sometime I would get ill and bring it all up.

When I tried to tell her that I couldn't eat the food she called me ungrateful and told me my parents would be glad to have something like this to eat. I doubted that. My parents liked eating rabbit and bannock, berries and potatoes just fine. But I didn't tell her that. Arguing would just get me into more trouble.

Another knock at the door. "Come and eat your breakfast," called a voice from the other side of the door. I got up and followed my landlady to the kitchen. There on the table was my breakfast—cereal, toast and milk.

While I was eating breakfast, the woman who was my landlady explained to me that they were going on a family outing. "Not too many more nice weekends before the snow comes," she said. "We're going to take advantage of this one." I could hear their two little boys playing downstairs in the basement. They were playing with the electric train set their father had set up down there. I was not allowed to go near it. I was also not allowed to play with their two boys without permission. I wondered about that sometime. I did not understand why they treated me so differently from the way they treated everyone else. I suspected they did not like me. The landlady's voice intruded on my thoughts.

"Drink up your milk now, and don't bother coming back until nine o'clock this evening. The house will be locked." These Christians sure don't trust Indians, I thought as I got up and took my dishes to the sink.

After breakfast, I wandered outside to the back yard. The landlord was already out there washing his car. I sat on the back steps and watched him. "Come over here and give me a hand with this," he called. So I did. When we were finished washing and waxing the car, he went back inside and soon they all came out. They seemed to be in a good mood, laughing and talking about the wild animal park. I got up and headed for the sidewalk and started walking down the street. I had nowhere to go, but I thought they would get mad if it looked like I was going to hang around the house all day. I was barely half a block from the house when they drove by. The parents were in front, looking straight ahead, the kids were sitting in the back, looking around. They waved as they went by. I waved back and smiled, trying to look happy.

I watched until the car turned the corner two blocks down the street, then I turned around and walked back to the house. I went into the back yard and stood on the backstep for awhile and finally sat down.

The back yard was separated by a tall picket fence from the yards on either side of it. There was also a garden at the back.

The neighbour's back door opened. A man and a woman followed by a little boy stepped outside. They did not see me. The man was dressed in shorts and a tee shirt, the woman in a bathing suit. They sat down on a couple of lawn chairs, which were placed around a small table. The little boy ran to the end of the yard, where there

45

was a swing and slide and a sand box full of toys. I looked back at the parents. They had been joined by a small black dog with short curly hair. He was sprawled on the ground between the two people, soaking up the sun. I got up from the steps and went a little closer to the fence so I would be out of sight. I did not want them to think I was spying on them. They might get mad at me. From where I now sat, I could hear them talking about the new car they were planning to buy. The man talked about a contract for playing hockey. This meant they could get a new car. He also had another job. This would take care of their other bills.

I thought about my parents and family at home. My dad had more than two jobs. He had to catch horses before he could do anything. This was a job in itself. Our horses could run very fast and jump fences. Then he had to drive them out to the bush so he could chop wood and haul it home, where he sawed it into small pieces so it would fit into our cook-stove. He also had to haul water. And hunt. He usually did this when he was out in the bush chopping wood. I could see him standing on top of a load of wood on the sleigh, or maybe walking beside it if it was really cold. It was better to keep moving on very cold days. There would usually be a rabbit or two and sometimes even three if he was lucky. We used to run outside to meet him and fight about who would carry the rabbits into the house to give to my mom. She was very good at cleaning and skinning rabbits. She had been doing it for years.

Too bad my dad couldn't get a job playing hockey, I thought. I was sure the folks back home who played hockey didn't get paid to do it. They just did it to be together and have fun. I had heard my dad telling a story to some people about a hockey game. They had cleared the ice on a section of the creek that runs through our reserve. A group of young fellows had got together to have a game. There were just about enough of them for two teams, but one of the teams was minus a goal tender. They managed to talk Leo, who didn't know how to skate, into putting on a pair of skates and being their goalie. Leo shoved some newspapers up each pantleg and wrapped them around his ankles and tied them up with twine. Two of his teammates supported him on either side and pulled him out to his goal. He managed, barely, to stay on his feet by propping himself up with the crude goalie stick someone had hastily nailed together for him. For a puck, they were using a freshly frozen piece of horse dropping they had picked up in someone's barn. Dad said these really smarted if they hit an unprotected spot. The other boys had chopped down suitably curved willow trees for hockey sticks.

Leo's team won the game. Ecstatic over their victory, they all rushed off to the fire, which was roaring beside the creek. They didn't notice Leo until someone started laughing and pointing at the rink. There was Leo, crawling across the ice on his hands and knees toward the fire, dragging his stick behind him.

I smiled remembering the story. Suddenly, I heard a car starting. I had forgottten about the people next door. While I had been thinking, or daydreaming as my teachers called it, the neighbours had moved back inside. Now they had come back out and were about to drive off in their car. I looked up at the sun and realized I had been sitting there daydreaming all morning. And now I was hungry.

Back home If you were hungry you just went somewhere to visit at mealtime and you would be sure to get fed. I decided to give it a try. I tried to think of someone I could go and visit. There was Allen, who lived across the street and was in my class at school. But he hadn't been very friendly to me. I decided not to go over there. A few houses down lived another kid who was in my class. His name was Robert. He had asked me if I wanted to come to the field beside their place and play football. I had wanted to but I didn't know how to play football, so I had declined the invitation.

I got up and walked down the street. When I reached their house I almost turned around but I was hungry. I thought it was a funny thing no one ever used their front door since it was closer to the street. They all used the back door. Our house at home only had one door so we had no choice.

I stood there trying to muster the courage to knock on the door. The screen door was the only obstacle between me and the food I could smell cooking inside. That spurred me on. I knocked and waited. I could hear voices and finally a very tall lady came to the door.

"Is Robert home?" I asked, hoping she would invite me in.

"Yes, he's in," she replied. "But he's having his dinner. Why don't you come back in half an hour or so? He should be finished by then." With that she closed the door and walked away. I felt embarrassed, thinking she must have known why I was there. Well I wouldn't try that again. I turned around and retraced my steps to the back yard of the house where I lived. It was then I noticed the carrots in the garden. Too dangerous, I decided, my landlady would notice if I took even one. I sat down by the fence and immediately fell asleep. I must have slept most of the afternoon, because when I awoke the neighbours were back. I could hear them talking on the other side of the fence. I got up and went over to the fence. There was an outside tap sticking out of the wall of the house. The landlady ran a hose from it to the garden to water those carrots. I thought of them again. My hunger had returned. It was more urgent now. I turned on the tap and let the water run over my arms and hands. It felt cool and refreshing. I cupped my hands and filled them up, stuck my face in the water and felt a tingle go all the way down to my toes. I was awake again. I dried myself off with my shirt sleeves. Then I went and sat back down in my spot. There I felt safe.

"Make mine kind of rare, I like it like that," said the woman. Suddenly I was blasted by the aroma of meat cooking over a fire. I knew the smell, having often eaten meat cooked over a fire. I was just drifting off on memories of home when the man next door yelled, "That damn dog!" Just then the dog came bounding around the corner of the fence and into the yard I was in. It was carrying a steak in its mouth. The man was not far behind. He came running around the fence, still carrying the huge fork he must have been using to turn the meat. So preoccupied with what was behind it that it totally ignored anything in front of it, the dog ran right into me. The dog and the man came to a dead stop.

"Well, hello there. I didn't think there was anyone home here," the man said to me.

"There isn't," I answered. "They went somewhere for the day. They're not going to be home until around nine o'clock."

"Do you live here?" he asked, seeming to have forgotten about the steak.

"Yes," I answered.

"Have you eaten yet?"

"No," I replied, not daring to look at the man.

"We were just going to eat. You could join us if you wanted to. Come on," he urged. I did not need much urging. He speared the steak the dog had dropped, turned around and started to walk back into his yard, his dog and me close behind.

I did not leave any of the huge steak they served me. I could barely move, but I somehow managed to put away a large helping of ice cream for dessert. It was the best meal I had eaten in a long time.

The man's name was Jake. It turned out that he played hockey for the Moose Jaw Canucks. He gave me a couple of tickets to the next game against the Regina Pats. I didn't go to the game but I hope they won.

On The Road

Bernelda Wheeler

My dad says it's a reserve road.
Car wheels drive on it,
But horses and wagons made it.
Albert says when he was a boy
Him and his friends used to make
Mini harnesses for gophers,
Then hitch them up to stones for wagons
And race them in the ruts.
But they got caught by an old man
Who scolded them
And they couldn't do it anymore.
Long John walks on the high ground
Between the ruts when he goes to town.
And he won't get out of the way of cars
So they have to drive around him.
If you half close your eyes,
And look at it from the top of a hill,
You can make believe it's two black snakes.
They even move if you imagine hard enough.
Sometimes it can be two rivers too.
Blind Bill used to sit against a fence post
Close to the road and sing in Cree
With his tin cup held high in both hands.
We put money in his cup.
Then he would say prayers.

It takes you to town.
And it brings you home.
It's almost like people that road.
Some days it gets mad and won't co-operate with cars.
But some days it acts real good.
Winter times it turns into a skating rink.
Some people can't drive on it,
But it's easy for Indians.
People say there's a good reason for that.
My dad says it's because it's a reserve road.

Phoebe's Trip To Mexico

Priscilla Settee

Phoebe lived in Cumberland House, a small village along the North Saskatchewan River. One day, she and her friend Seraphine were sitting at the kitchen table drinking apple/cinnamon tea when Phoebe said to Seraphine, who was much older, "Let's go to Mexico!"

Seraphine said, "Do you know where Mexico is?"

Phoebe replied, "Of course, it's over by Vancouver. Why don't I ask Kookoom if I can go?"

After finishing their tea they agreed to meet the following day to discuss their plans. Phoebe's Kookoom was a little cautious when she first listened to the plan but she finally agreed to let Phoebe go in Seraphine's care.

When Seraphine heard the news she clapped her hands with glee and said, "Let's plan to leave after you are out of school. That's only two months from now." With that, they started to prepare for the trip. They sent for passports, and checked with Doris, the community health nurse, as to which needles they required, and they asked Uncle Angus to care for Seraphine's hounds, Atim and Roger.

Two months later, Uncle Angus drove them to Saskatoon, where they boarded a big jet which flew them to Tijuana, a northern Mexican town. Phoebe had never been this far from home before and she held Seraphine's hand the whole time.

As the big jet came down to land, Phoebe looked out of the window and caught her breath. Spread out below, for as far as she could see, was sand.

"That is called a desert," Seraphine said, looking over her shoulder, "and look Phoebe, there's the ocean."

Phoebe had never seen anything like this in her entire life. The ocean didn't look at all like the big lakes at home. It shone and sparkled like a million diamonds in the bright sunshine.

The jet bounced a couple of times as it came down on the runway. Phoebe could hardly wait to get off, there was so much to see. She was so busy looking at everything and listening to the strange language that she was not even aware that they had walked out of the airport and taken a cab into the city, until Seraphine, who had been to Mexico before, patted Phoebe's hand and reminded her that it was time to eat lunch.

Phoebe looked around. They were in the middle of a little square. "Over there," Seraphine pointed to a sign that said Henrico's Restaurant. Henrico, who remembered Seraphine from her last visit, beamed broadly when they entered the restaurant, which was little more than an extended kitchen.

"Hola," he said.

"Hola," replied Seraphine.

"Hola," said Phoebe after realizing that this must be a greeting of sorts.

"It means hello," whispered Seraphine.

Henrico sat down to visit with them while they ate their meal of fish and tortillas. When they were finished they paid for their lunch, thanked Henrico and set out to find a place to spend the night.

After walking for a few blocks they came across a cozy little thatch-roofed palapa.

"This looks like a good place to stay," said Seraphine as she knocked on the door.

"Ay quatros, Senora?" Seraphine asked the lady who answered the door.

"Si," said the braided Senora, beckoning them to come in and showing them a room with sunshine streaming through the windows.

"Gracias Senora," Seraphine said, "this is just what we need." Phoebe nodded in agreement, thinking how much the Senora looked like her Aunty Edith back home in Cumberland House.

The Senora smiled, "De Nada Chicatita," she said, closing the door behind her.

They unpacked their suitcases, shooed the mosquitoes out and collapsed on the straw mattresses on the wooden beds.

"Oh, I'm so tired," Seraphine said, shutting her eyes.

Phoebe, with her hands folded behind her head, was staring at the ceiling, planning a letter to her Kookoom back in Cumberland House. "Do you suppose we could go to the pyramids tomorrow?" asked Phoebe.

"Sure," said Seraphine, who had visions of tortillas and mangoes dancing in her head.

The next morning as the sun crept over the rubber trees, parakeets poked fun at the two late-risers. As they splashed water on their faces they heard someone call out "Hugos."

Seraphine said, "Phoebe, would you like some juice? I'll run down and get us some." A few minutes later she returned with two bags of fresh orange juice.

"Dee-licious," said Phoebe, puckering her mouth. After a long lazy breakfast of fried plantanos, rice and fresh mangoes, they set out for the pryamids.

Phoebe had done her homework before she travelled, so while they gazed at the mysterious stone structures, built thousands of years ago by their Aztec Indian cousins, she told what she knew of the stories and meanings associated with the buildings. Seraphine was truly impressed by the knowledge of such a young person.

They spent several days at the ruins. On the fifth day, Phoebe said, "Let's go to the mountains. Henrico told me of an Indian village over there," she said, pointing with her lips in the direction of the mountains. "Okay," said Seraphine, who by this time was starting to envy the energy of the younger traveller. That night, in the glow of a tiny candle, Phoebe began to weave a story on paper to her aged Kookoom away back home in Cumberland House. Finally when all the birds had sung themselves to sleep, she put away her paper and pencil and fell into a deep sleep.

When morning arrived, they packed a few clothes, caught a bus and headed off into the mountains. They chugged along at a hedgehog's pace for a whole day and when the bus finally stopped they found themselves in a tiny Indian village nestled high in the mountains. Directly in front of them an Indian family stared at the two travellers as they climbed out of the bus.

"Hola," said Phoebe.

"Hola," said the mother, extending her hand. The children peered around their father with flirtatious shoe-button eyes. "We have heard all over the valley about you, our Canadian cousins. We would be happy if you would come to our home."

"We would be honoured," said Seraphine, and they set off with the family, joined by others as they walked through the little village.

As they arrived at the one-room house they were met by many mouth-watering smells. "I'm starving," Phoebe thought as the father offered the two travellers fried iguana. Phoebe knew it was a lizard-like creature, but she thought it tasted a bit like chicken.

Dusk was approaching by the time they finished their meal. Phoebe looked out the window and could see lights coming from the windows of tiny houses nestled in the mountains. A warm feeling came over her, the soft light on the old wooden table and the family gathered around talking and laughing reminded her of home. When the Father began telling stories Phoebe's eyes filled with tears.

"What is the matter, Chicatita?" The man stopped his storytelling.

"You look like my Uncle Angus," whispered Phoebe. "He is a storyteller, too."

The man smiled gently, "Ah," he said. "Our stories, like yours, have been with us for centuries. It is our hope that they will continue."

"That is what Uncle Angus hopes, too," smiled Phoebe.

"At a certain time of the year, when the sun moves north, we celebrate that which gives us life, corn. A good crop means an abundant year and lots of food for our people. The celebration begins with music played on a marimba. Men and women dance around carrying the corn sticks while the men sing. It is our way of honouring the Creator who gives us the corn that gives us life."

The stories flowed along so smoothly that soon it was time to go to sleep. That night after the candles were blown out and everyone was tucked away in bed, Phoebe fell asleep with her head on Seraphine's arm and dreamed about the corn festival.

The next morning before anyone else was up, Phoebe tiptoed out, and under the shade of a eucalyptus tree, continued her letter to Kookoom. It had been a few weeks since she left home and Phoebe was beginning to miss roasted muskrat and bannock and sitting around the old stove with Uncle Angus, but most of all she missed her Kookoom. She wondered whether Uncle Angus was at the summer camp on the lake by now. She remembered the evening cry of the loon and the taste of fried jackfish. She thought about the chilly evening, the crackling woodstoves and the smell of stretched beaverskins hanging on the walls. Mexico was a beautiful place, but she missed home.

Kookoom received her letter three weeks later. The day it arrived Uncle Angus tore it open while Kookoom waited with moist eyes for him to read it to her.

"Dear Kookoom," it began. Uncle Angus read about the countryside, the desert, the pyramids, the corn festival and the stories. "The people down here really look and think like us, Kookoom, and when we visit we eat mangoes and iguana, a lizard-like creature." At that point the old woman nearly fainted. "Mammaskatz," she said, putting her hand over her mouth. "I will be home in a few weeks, save some jackfish for me, kiss Uncle Angus. I miss you very much."

Back in Mexico, Phoebe and Seraphine spent the next few weeks helping their new family with the corn garden. The evenings were spent in the little house visiting and exchanging stories. It seemed like their lives had never been thousands of miles apart. Seraphine learned how to weave cloth and Phoebe tried her hand at pottery. Seraphine showed the children how to do beadwork in Cumberland House patterns.

Soon the time had come for the Canadian cousins to return home. On the morning of their departure, the family cooked them a special breakfast, special because they had iguanas and mangoes. They gave them each a handwoven woolen poncho and other gifts made of silver for Kookoom and Uncle Angus back in Cumberland.

It was difficult to say goodbye, so they decided to say, "See you soon" instead and that they would come back to visit some more. They exchanged hugs and kisses until the bus was ready to leave. Seraphine and Phoebe jumped on the bus which would take them back to Tijuana enroute to Saskatoon where Uncle Angus would meet them and drive them home to Cumberland House.

A Feather Story:
The Legend of the Laser Queen

Darlene R. Frenette

The laser bird did not want to die, but it seemed to have no choice, so it let go. It was able to do this only after a bitter struggle and the record of its battle was left imprinted in its feathers. It is a universal battle. The laser bird's feather, which holds this story, still exists, encircled by emerald guards in the star palace at Sirius. The story is about a desert warrior woman who became known as the

Laser Queen. The legend will always begin this way...

A long time ago, in a faraway galaxy, there was a brilliant blue planet with white, wispy mists encircling it. The most powerful creatures who lived there were torn apart by great inner wars and it was not known whether the planet would survive the strain of the battles being fought.

The wisest leaders in all their lands gathered in planetary councils to see if a way could be found to stop the great wars. They could not agree because each was afraid that his own people would lose what power they had left on the planet. So everything stayed the same and the fighting grew worse.

Meanwhile, an unusual disturbance occurred in the solar system. It caused a devastating earthquake, which tore a giant crack in the earth's surface from the north pole, all around the other side, to the north pole again. Out of the dark depths of the great chasm arose a lethal, greyish-green fog that would not go away. It prevented the people on each side of the planet from seeing and communicating with each other. Around the outer layer of fog, a swirling blue-green mist erupted in violent electrical storms. It divided the planet in half and the highest technology that both sides possessed could not penetrate the menacing fog. After a time, the fog threatened to spread and cover the entire planet.

The finest scientists and power minds on both sides travelled vast distances to meet in secret councils to see if they could find some way to penetrate the fog, but to no avail. Many brave warrior minds on both sides became desperate to bridge the chasm on the planet's surface. As the mist spread, the world became darker and darker. The great fog barrier created such difficulties for scientists that they despaired. To make things worse, many leaders on each side of the planet wished only to conquer those on the other side. The people were afraid, so again and again the finest minds gathered to explore what could be done. But the plans they made were so dangerous that no one dared carry them out.

Then a strange thing happened. A mysterious warrior woman appeared before the council and told the leaders that she would journey through the mist and fog of the great chasm and bring back the secret of bridging the world. The only condition was that others be allowed to go with her. She told them of an isolated desert people who had rare and special powers that were needed for the journey, but she worried that they had to be carefully prepared.

The leaders were surprised. They had never heard a desert woman in a planetary council before. But time was running out and they had no choice. They chose warriors from across the lands, including some from the desert regions, and they began a long and perilous training. Out of all who were chosen, only the warrior woman and two other desert women had the vision and the courage to make the attempt.

The council leaders gathered at the edge of a desert to observe the three warriors enter the mist as they began their long journey to the other side. They soon disappeared behind hills of sand in the stormy mists. After a while, however, one of the women lost her courage in the fierce flashes of mist, fearing for her life, so she turned around and went back to her family and friends. The other woman turned away, too, and was never seen again. The warrior woman searched for the others in the darkening mist, but finding no one, she went on herself.

The journey was frightening now. The path was steep with perilous rock looming out of the fog. Terrifying creatures lurched from masses of swirling clouds. They tried to attack her from all sides. Some of the creatures had long beaks and they tore skin from her body as she struggled through invisible barriers. The further she advanced into the fog the more vicious the monsters became. Some had gleaming black eyes like beetles and huge, dripping mouths with dagger-like teeth that slashed at her face. Sometimes, vague forms behind rocks threw evil things at her and though she bled and hurt from the wounds, she pressed on with her journey.

Suddenly, when she felt she could stand no more, the dark and evil creatures melted into the mists and disappeared. A kind-looking medicine woman stepped out from behind a rock and smiled gently at her. She spoke soothing words to the now tired warrior and commended her for striving so hard. Others, who looked like friends, joined the woman and then they told her that it was time for her to go home. The warrior woman gazed into the eyes of the kind-looking woman and saw that they were icy cold and hard. She knew they were only monsters trying to stop her journey. She turned away from them and struggled onward.

Finally, she broke into a clearing in the mist and in the centre of the clearing she saw something wonderful. Three huge rocks the size of trees stood equidistant from one another. A soft, crimson mist floated around the rocks and a golden shaft of sunlight illuminated the whole area. It was the first time she had glimpsed the blue sky and light from the sun since the start of the awful journey. She approached the black chrysolite rocks and found that each had golden inscriptions etched into the surface. These inscriptions were instructions and secrets for the first three warriors to penetrate the mist. She was the first warrior to successfully make the crossing. It seemed that each warrior had a special task. She could only read the tasks meant for her because not until two more warriors made the journey would the three together hold the secret of bridging the mist so that both sides of the planet could communicate once more. She wrote down all the secrets that were meant for her from the first, second and third rock and then she knew it was time to leave.

On her way back through the treacherous fog, she saw the same monsters and evil forms but they no longer frightened her. Mirages of her friends with hateful eyes no longer troubled her. She knew that no one could harm her. The jagged rock and steep cliffs were still dangerous but now nothing could hurt her, for a new and powerful force surged through her body. When monsters came too close she would raise her hand and from it would stream an intense ray of light which would scatter them in the mist. The hurtful things they threw at her no longer had any effect. It was because of this that she came to be known as the Laser Queen.

She stepped out of the mist one day, battle-worn and weary but happy, and once again she stood before the planetary council. She presented them with the gift of what she had seen on her journey and of what she knew about bridging the mists. The leaders did not know what to think or say. Some were wise and listened carefully, but most were angry and some were jealous. Many laughed at her and told her that the mist had taken away her reason and they could not believe her story. It did not matter to her anymore because she knew that until two more warriors could return from the journey, her work for the great council was done. Fearlessly, the Laser Queen slipped quietly into the mists and went to the other side of the planet to search for warriors who could make the journey and who would return to help teach both sides how to destroy the fog and cross the great chasm in the world.

That is how the legend of the Laser Queen began, long ago, as it is recorded in the laser bird's feather. There are other feathers with more of this story but they are held in other galaxies many light years away.

Lean Man, Edward Poitras

about **Lean Man**:

*"**Lean Man** was the beginning of a series of works on paper exploring the image of the headdress. It became a very frustrating process of eliminating excess image. The final works in this series had more to do with the essence of frustration. A non-objective and geometric relationship in harmony."*

Allen Sapp

A full-blooded Cree Indian, Allen Sapp was born in 1929 on the Red Pheasant Reservation, Saskatchewan. He was sickly as a child and had very little school education. Although he is now internationally known, fame has changed him little.

A deeply religious man, he believes that God and happiness are one. He feels close to God when he is outdoors, especially in the woods. He likes to sit alone studying the world around him. He never sketches, but relies on his photographic memory.

Allen Sapp has recorded in oils and acrylics the life of his people on the reservation as he remembers it. "I put it down so it doesn't get lost and people will be able to see and remember."

"Painting is a feeling," he says, "just like Indian music is a feeling. I can't write a story or tell one in the white man's language so I tell what I want to say with my painting."

about **Going Visiting**:

"People like to visit their friends. When I was a boy they used to take their open sleigh and horses and the man always drove. He had a whip but he didn't hurt the horses, it was only to make them go. The Esquoio would be on the sleigh and a nice warm blanket on top of the hay and she would sit on top of the blanket and cover herself with part of the blanket. The horse would eat some of the hay later"

about **Playing Around**:

"Some of the kids who had skates would play hockey at the slough in back of my Grandfather's house a long time ago. Sometimes kids would play without skates if they didn't have any and if they didn't have a puck they would use a piece of frozen horse droppings. If their hands got cold they would warm them up by the fire."

66   *Going Visiting*, Allen Sapp

Playing Around, Allen Sapp

67

Michael Lonechild

Michael Lonechild has been quoted as saying that he could paint before he could talk.

A Cree, born in 1955 on the White Bear Reservation, Saskatchewan, Michael still lives on the reserve, with his wife Gwen Little Chief and their two young sons.

Michael is essentially a self-taught artist. His work has been enthusiastically received and has brought him a measure of financial success.

His agent says, "Lonechild himself does not verbalize his work." But in an article in **The Beaver** magazine (Summer, 1980), he did make this statement about his purpose in painting, "I like to paint on the reserve. Soon it will be changed. In 10 years, this will all be gone. And I like to paint the old people. But they don't always like me to do it. Usually I have to paint them from memory."

The article went on to describe his method:

"Lonechild prefers acrylic paints on canvas and canvas board as his medium. He takes long walks over the reserve, familiarizes himself with history through books and periodicals, and listens to stories told by the 'elders' as to how it was in the past. Armed with these impressions and information, he works at home, combining his sources with an imagination of his own."

70   *Making My Dad's Tea*, Michael Lonechild

Just Visiting, Michael Lonechild 71

Raymond McCallum

about **Harvest Moon**:

"**Harvest Moon** *was done from the experience and perspective of most Indian people. The meal, consisting of grease bannock, macaroni soup and crushed chokecherries, are the staples that many Indian people grow up with. This food is also often served at Indian feasts. Most people enjoy it more than a 'fancy' meal because it is very filling and satisfying.*"

Henry Beaudry was born in 1921 on Poundmaker Reservation, Saskatchewan, but transferred to the Mosquito Reservation in 1948, after returning from the War.

From 1941-45 Henry served in the Armed Forces. He participated in the invasion of Sicily and in 1944 was taken prisoner in Italy, but escaped and made his way to Holland. "I had my eagle feather with me all through the War," he tells, "but lost it the day before I was taken prisoner."

Henry began painting in 1959. He had been working for the CNR, but got pneumonia and was laid off. He decided he had to do something, so started sketching.

Henry was married when he was 18 and his wife 13. They had six children of their own plus two more they raised.

about **Bald Eagle Moon**:

"Before I was school age, I dreamed of the eagle. He was white, with spots. A voice told me I was going to have a hard road, but at the end it would be happy. I always think of that eagle.

"When I was about 19, we were working near Alsask, picking stones. We were camped on the side of the road. A flock of golden eagles came down and sat on fenceposts, just like crows. I was happy seeing them.

"We don't kill eagles. They're sacred. We only use their feathers for the dance. They must hang down in front of the dancer.

"This eagle just came to me. I couldn't get away from it, so I just painted it."

74   *Harvest Moon*, Raymond McCallum

Bald Eagle Moon, Henry Beaudry

75

A Mountain Legend

Jordan Wheeler

The school bus drove into a small summer camp at the base of a towering mountain. Boys and girls between the ages of eight and twelve, who had signed up for the three-day camping trip, poured out of the bus. Following instructions from counsellors, they began hurriedly preparing their camp as the sunset dripped over the rock walls towering above them. For many, it was their first time away from the city, which they could still see far off in the distance. Tents were put up and sleeping bags unrolled before the last of the twilight rays gave way to the darkness of night.

Roasting marshmallows around a large campfire, the young campers listened intently to stories told by the counsellors. Behind the eager campers, the caretaker of the camp sat on the ground, himself listening to the stories.

As the night grew old, the younger children wearily found their way to their tents, so that by midnight only the twelve-year-olds remained around the fire with one counsellor and the caretaker. Their supply of stories seemingly exhausted, they sat in silence watching the glowing embers of the once fiery blaze shrink into red-hot ash.

"The moon is rising," announced the caretaker in a low, even voice.

All eyes looked up to the glow surrounding the jagged peaks of the mountain. The blackness of the rock formed an eerie silhouette against the gently lit sky.

The caretaker's name was McNabb. He had lived close to the mountain all his life and knew many of the stories the mountain had seen. He threw his long, black braided hair over his shoulders, drew the collar of his faded jean jacket up against the crisp mountain air, and spoke.

"There is a legend about this mountain once told by the mountain itself," he said, paused for a moment, then continued. "People claim that long ago it told of a young boy who tried to climb up to an eagle's nest which rested somewhere among the many cliffs. He was from a small camp about a day's journey from here and when he was twelve years old, he thought he was ready to become a warrior. His father disagreed, saying he was too young and too small. But the boy was stubborn and one morning before dawn he sneaked out of his family's teepee and set off on foot toward the mountain. There were no horses in North America in his time. They were brought later by the Europeans.

"It took most of the day for him to reach the mountain. The next morning, he set out to find an eagle and seek a vision from the mighty bird, as that was the first step in becoming a warrior. But as he was climbing up the rock cliffs to a nest, he fell to his death, releasing a terrible cry that echoed from the mountain far out across the land. The legend says the boy's spirit still wanders the mountain today."

A coyote howled in the distance and the campers jumped.

"Is it true?" asked one of the boys, with worry and fear in his voice.

"Some people say so, and they also say you can still hear his scream every once in a while."

All around the dying fire, eyes were straining up at the menacing rock peaks. The caretaker McNabb, however, wasn't looking at the mountain, he was watching one of the young campers. He was an Indian boy, smaller than the others, with short braided hair that fell down his back. The boy was gazing up at the mountain, his curiosity obviously blended with fear. Turning his head, his eyes met those of McNabb. For a fleeting moment, they locked stares, then

McNabb relaxed, a knowing expression spreading over his face, while the boy continued to stare at him, wide-eyed and nervous.

There were small discussions around the fire, debating the story's truth before the counsellor told them it was time for sleep. Both tired and excited, they retreated to their tent and crawled into their sleeping bags.

The boy Jason lay in a tent he shared with two other boys, who lay talking in the dark. As Jason waited for the heat of his body to warm his sleeping bag, he thought of that long ago boy. He felt a closeness to him and imagined himself in his place.

"Hey Jason, why don't you climb up that mountain tomorrow morning and try to catch an eagle?" It was Ralph, who was against the far wall of the tent on the other side of Barry.

"Why?" asked Jason.

"You're Indian aren't you? Don't you want to become a warrior?"

True, Jason was Indian, but he knew nothing of becoming a warrior. He had spent all his life in the city. All he knew of his heritage was what his grandmother told him from time to time, which wasn't much. He had been to three pow wows in his life, all at a large hall not far from his house, but he never learned very much. His time was spent eating hot dogs, drinking pop, and watching the older boys play pool in the adjoining rooms. Little as he knew though, he wanted Ralph and Barry to think he knew a lot.

"No. It's not time for me to be a warrior yet," he told them.

"Why not?" Barry asked.

"It just isn't, that's all," Jason said, not knowing a better answer.

"You're chicken, you couldn't climb that mountain if you tried," Ralph charged.

"I'm not chicken! I could climb that mountain, no problem. It just isn't time yet."

"You're chicken," Ralph said again.

"Go to sleep!" boomed a voice across the campground.

Ralph gave out three chicken clucks and rolled over to sleep.

Jason lay there in mild anger. He hated being called a chicken and if the counsellor hadn't shouted at that moment, he would have given Ralph a swift punch. But Ralph was right, the mountain did scare him.

With his anger subsiding, he drifted into a haunting sleep, filled with dreams. Dreams the wind swept through the camp, gently spreading the mountain spirit's stories throughout. A coyote's piercing howl echoed down the rocky cliffs, making Jason flinch in his sleep.

The following morning, Ralph, Barry, and Jason were the first ones up. As they emerged from the tent into the chilled morning air, their attention was immediately grasped by the huge rock peaks looming high above. Ralph's searching eyes spanned the mountain. A light blanket of mist enveloped its lower reaches.

Pointing up he said, "See that ledge up there?" Jason and Barry followed Ralph's arm to a cliff along one of the rock walls just above the tree line. "I bet you can't get to it," he dared Jason.

"I could so," Jason responded.

"Prove it," Ralph said.

Jason was trapped and he knew it. If he said no, he would be admitting he was scared. And there was another challenge in Ralph's voice, unsaid, but Jason heard it. Ralph was daring him to prove himself an Indian. Jason had lived his whole life in a city on cement ground and among concrete mountains where climbing was as easy as walking up stairs or pressing an elevator button. To prove to Ralph and himself that he was Indian, Jason had to climb to that ledge. He knew that mountain climbing could end a life. And there were wild animals he might have to deal with. How was he supposed to react? How would he react? He was afraid. He didn't want to go. But if he didn't?

"What's the matter?" Ralph taunted. "Indian scared?"

At that point, Jason decided he would face the mountain and he would reach that ledge. "Okay," he conceded.

At first, the climbing was easy, but his progress became slow and clumsy as he got higher up. Struggling over uneven ground and through trees, he came across a large flat rock. In need of a rest, he sat down and looked down at the campground he had left right after breakfast an hour ago. He could see bodies scurrying about. If they hadn't noticed by now that he was missing, he thought, no doubt they would soon.

Looking up, he could just see the ledge above the tree line. It wasn't much further, he thought. He could get to it, wave down at the camp to show he had made it, and be back in time for lunch. Raising himself up, he started to climb again, marching through the trees and up the steep slope, over the rough terrain.

A few moments later he heard a loud howl that seemed to come from somewhere above. At first, he thought it was a coyote, but it sounded more like a human. Nervously, he kept going.

In the camp, Ralph and Barry were getting ready to help prepare lunch. McNabb was starting a fire not far away. They, too, heard the howl.

"I never knew coyotes did that during the day," Ralph said to Barry.

Overhearing them, McNabb responded, "That was no coyote."

Half an hour later, Jason stood just above the tree line. The ledge, his goal, was thirty feet above, but what lay ahead was treacherous climbing, nearly straight up the rock wall. He scrutinized the rock face, planned his route and began to pick his way up the last stretch.

The mountain saw the boy encroaching and whispered a warning to the wind sweeping strongly down its face as it remembered a similar event long ago. Jason felt the wind grow stronger, driving high-pitched sound into his ears. Gripping the rock harder, he pulled himself up a bit at a time. The wind seemed to be pushing him back. But he felt something else, too, something urging him on.

When he was about twenty feet up the rock face, with his feet firmly on a small ledge, he chanced a look down between his legs. He could see that if he slipped, he would plummet straight down for that twenty feet and after hitting the rocks below, he would tumble a great distance further. He knew it would spell death and for a split second, he considered going back down. But once again he felt an outside force pushing him to go on. It gave him comfort and courage. His face reddened, his heart pounded, and beads of sweat poured from him as he inched his way higher. Straight above, an eagle flew in great circles, slowly moving closer to Jason and the ledge.

Far down the mountain the search for Jason was well underway, but the counsellors had no way of knowing where he was, as Ralph and Barry hadn't told. McNabb also knew where Jason was, but he, too, remained silent.

An eight-year-old girl in the camp lay quietly in her tent, staring up through the screen window at the sky. The search for Jason had been tiring and she had come back for a rest. She was watching a cloud slowly change shape when a large black bird flew by high above. Out of curiosity, she unzipped the tent door and went outside to get a better look. She watched the bird fly in smaller and smaller circles, getting closer and closer to the mountain. She took her eyes off the bird for a moment to look at the huge rock wall, and there, high above the trees and only a few feet below a ledge, she saw the boy climbing. Right away she knew the boy was in danger. After hesitating for a moment, she ran to tell a counsellor.

Jason paused from climbing, just a few feet below the ledge. He was exhausted and the insides of his hands were raw, the skin having been scraped off by the rough rock. The ledge was so close.

He pulled himself up to it, placing his feet inside a crack in the rock for support. Reaching over the edge, he swept one arm along the ledge, found another spot for his feet, hoisted his body up, rolled onto the ledge and got to his feet. There, an arm's length away on the ledge, were two young eagles in a large nest. For several minutes he just remained there looking at the baby eagles. He had never seen an eagle's nest before. He was so interested in the two young eagles he didn't notice the mother eagle circling high overhead, nor did he hear her swoop down towards him and her nest. She landed in front of him, spread her wings, and let out a loud screech. Jason was so terrified, he instinctively jumped and in doing so, lost his balance. Both feet stepped out into air as he grabbed the rock.

His hands clung desperately to the ledge as the sharp rock dug into his skin. He looked down and saw his feet dangling in the air. The wind swung him, making it impossible to get his feet back on the rock where they had been moments earlier. A coyote howled and Jason's terror grew. Again he looked down at the rocks below. Tears began streaming down his face. He didn't want to die. He wished he had never accepted Ralph's dare. He could picture them coming up the mountain, finding his dead body among the rocks, and crying over him. He began crying out loud and heard it echoing off the rock. Or he thought it was an echo. He stopped and listened. There was more crying, but not from him. Again he felt the presence of something or someone else. The wind swirled in and whispered to Jason the mountain's legend.

Though running swiftly, the boy Muskawashee had paced himself expertly for the day's journey. He would arrive at the base of the mountain far earlier than he had expected and would have plenty of daylight left to catch his supper and find a spot for a good night's sleep. Though small and having seen only twelve summers, his young body was strong. He would be able to reach the mountain in only two runs, pausing in between to catch a rabbit for lunch.

As his powerful legs moved him gracefully across the prairie, he thought back to the conversation with his father the day before. He had explained how most of his friends were already in preparation for manhood and he felt he was ready also. He did not want to wait for the next summer.

When some of his friends came back later that day from a successful buffalo hunt, he decided he would go to the mountain alone and seek a vision from the eagle.

He knew he would have to rise before the sun to get out of camp without being seen.

When he reached the base of the mountain, the sun was still well above the horizon. He sat down in a sheltered area for a rest. He decided this was where he would sleep for the night.

After a few minutes, he got up and made himself a trap for a rabbit and planted it. After laying the trap, he wandered off to look for some berries to eat while preparing his mind for the following day when he would climb the mountain. After some time, he returned to his trap and found a rabbit in it. He skinned it with a well-sharpened stone knife he had brought with him, and built a fire to cook his meal. He would keep the fire burning all night to keep away the wild animals while he slept.

Finishing his meal, he thanked the creator for his food and safe journey and prayed for good fortune in his quest for a vision. Then he lay down in the soft moss and fell asleep to the music of the coyote's howls and the whispering wind.

The next morning, he awoke to the sun's warming shine. The still-smouldering fire added an aroma of burnt wood to the fresh air. He again prayed to the creator for good fortune in his quest for a vision and for a safe journey up the mountain. When he finished, he looked up, high above, and saw eagles flying to and from a rock ledge. This would be his goal.

Half an hour later, he stood where the trees stopped growing and the bare rock began. His powerful body had moved steadily through the trees even though he wasn't used to uphill running. Without resting, he continued his climb, knowing he would have to be careful ahead. The mountain could be dangerous and its spirit could be evil.

As he pulled himself up the face of the rock, he heard the mountain spirit warning him to stay away. Its voice was the whispering wind, which grew stronger and seemed to be trying to push him back. With determination, Muskawashee climbed. High above, the powerful eagle circled its nest.

Just five feet below the ledge, Muskawashee paused. He was dripping with perspiration from fighting the wind and the mountain. Though scared, he would not let fear overcome him. His desire for manhood was stronger. His hands were hurting and covered in blood from the climb, but he reached out again. After several scrabbling attempts, he was able to grab hold of the ledge and pull himself up onto the narrow, flat edge. Eye to eye with two baby eagles, he stopped. He felt great pride and relief in having reached his goal and stood there savouring those feelings. He didn't hear the approach of the mother eagle. As she landed on the ledge in front of him, she let out a loud screech and spread her wings wide. Muskawashee was startled, stepped back and lost his footing. A gust of wind shoved him further and he could feel his body in the air as he tried to get a foot back on the rock. He grabbed the edge, but his arms were trembling and he could not pull himself back up. His fingers ached and began slipping from the edge. Knowing he would soon fall, he began whimpering. He looked up, into the eyes of the eagle. One day, he thought to himself, he would be back.

His fingers let go and he fell, releasing a loud, terrifying scream that echoed from the mountain, far out across the land, and down through time.

McNabb and one of the counsellors left the camp when the eight-year-old girl told them what she had seen. Both experienced hikers and mountain-climbers, they were able to cover the distance in a third of the time it took Jason. When they heard the scream, they quickened their pace. Minutes later, they reached the edge of the tree line and looked up at the ledge.

Jason, who had been hanging there for several minutes, also heard the scream and looked down into the eyes of Muskawashee as he fell. Jason felt the tension in his fingers, but sensed there were greater forces keeping him hanging there, perhaps the mountain itself was hanging on to him. Whatever it was, Jason remained high above McNabb and the counsellor, who were watching from the tree line. The wind died down and the eagle stepped back, making room for him on the ledge. Jason hoisted a foot back onto the ledge and tried again to haul himself onto the shelf.

Suddenly, he saw Muskawashee standing on the ledge, extending a hand down to him. Jason grabbed his hand and Muskawashee pulled. The two boys faced one another, looking into each other's eyes. The descendent gaining pride in being Indian, and the ancestor completing the quest he had begun hundreds of years earlier. A powerful swirl of wind swept Muskawashee away, leaving Jason alone before the eagle's nest. Jason reached down and picked up a feather out of the nest.

Below him stood the counsellor and McNabb. They had witnessed Jason's rescue.

"Who was that other kid up there?" asked the counsellor in disbelief.

McNabb smiled and answered. "Muskawashee. He will wander this mountain no more." Then, unravelling a long line of heavy rope he said, "Come on, let's get Jason down."

Naska

John Cuthand

Her home was the deep water pools of the South Saskatchewan River. Here among the water plants, rocks and sandbars she passed the day and avoided the only enemy she ever knew—the bright burning sun. She hunted alone and without remorse, for such is the way of the big northern pike.

Her name was Naska. She was in her prime, weighing over thirty-five pounds and stretching almost a yard. Her shining, well-muscled body was white on the bottom, a mottled green and white along the sides and dark green on top. Her mouth was a maze of needle-sharp teeth. Smaller fish avoided her. And only the hard-shelled painted turtle could afford to ignore her approach.

When the hot summer sun drove her into the deepest reaches of the river, she would hover, her fins circling, facing the current a foot or so above the bottom. It was here, in these long hours, that the waters told her stories. The river sang as it flowed over and around the deep water rocks. It spoke in the soft rustle of the water weeds and in the gurgle and murmur of water pouring around the few scattered boulders breaking the glassy surface.

The voice said, "I am the ancient daughter of ice mountain, born when the freezing sky allowed him dominion over the south. I am the blood of ice mountain, born from his death before the warming sky. I am ancient and I am mystery. I am swift-flowing water. I am Saskatchewan."

In the black of the late night she rose with the morning star. She fed until the star was high and fading. When the first rays of the shimmering sun cast long shadows, she herself was like a shadow sinking into her deep water pools. She surfaced with the setting of the sun, fed, then slid deeper when the night became black.

On cloudy days she ranged beyond her familiar haunts. In the fall, with the gradual cooling of the water, her range extended further still. In winter, when the ice sealed off the surface and the sun no longer warmed the water, she roamed as she pleased. She much preferred the colder water. In mid-summer she was sluggish, but that was also the time when the river sang to her.

One time it told her ice mountain had never been entirely defeated by the warming sky. "He rules still in one quarter of the sun's cycle. He covers me with his cloak and speaks to me in the booming thunder of my cracking ice mantle. He is father. In his death I was born. In his rebirth, I die. I am ancient but he is ageless."

In the time of the full moon Naska would rise and seek different prey. The moon's glow concealed her, but she could see them. They were the night creatures that live between water and land. For them the beckoning, seemingly peaceful waters held terror. Quick, violent death came with a splash and a swirl of black water. Where a gosling or a baby muskrat once swam, all that remained was an expanding ripple.

The big fish did not think in terms of right and wrong. Hunger, insatiable hunger, drove her and she killed only to live.

Among her moonlit prey the story spread of a water demon in the form of an enormous fish. The story was told in the haunting lonely laughter of the loons, the croaking chorus of the frightened frogs, and the chatterings of the milling ducks. The moonlight sighting of a long, shining back lolling over the water drove them further down the sandy bank away from that terrible place. The hunted lived in fear and they feared her most of all. If Naska knew of their fear, she didn't care. Generations of her kind before her and from her had ruled and would rule the river's waters. For the river in its mysterious way had willed it so.

She had been the mother of many. Perhaps some were among her kill, for the female pike takes no part in the raising of her young. Perhaps one or two would grow to her size if they survived the slaughter of the first years. One and one alone, however, was destined to become mistress of the river. The river in its way had willed it so. Naska was the survivor and heir of a mother who once ruled these waters as she did. This she did not know. She knew only that the river was her home and the river's spirit her sole benefactor.

One night, when the autumn moon was full and the great fish was on the hunt, a wandering band of antelope came to the river's edge. They waded out into the shallows and were drinking their fill, when their sharp-eyed leader spied a great shining back coming toward them. He watched intently, expecting an enormous snake, for snakes were creatures they knew well. A great finned tail curved upward, then sliced down, scarcely breaking the surface. "This is no snake," thought the antelope, "it is a creature solely bound to the water spirit."

The great fish felt a curious pulse from the shallows and veered toward it. This was not the fluttering sound of webbed feet, her usual prey. It was the feel of something large, many large creatures.

The antelope, alert as always, sensed that something very alien was close. They stiffened, raising their heads to sniff the wind. Only the leader gazed at the smooth, flowing water directly in front of them.

Naska followed the river bottom and rose as it rose. She came as close as boldness could take her before caution and the rising river bottom forced her off.

The leader was the first to notice the ruffled water above the shallow-running fish. The V-shaped wake came directly toward them, then moved away in a sharp curve. The antelope were nervous but their curiosity got the better of them. They watched in fascination as the dark shadow beneath the now churning water glided by, first one way then another, more slowly and closer with every pass.

Naska could not see straight ahead, because her eyes were on either side of her head. Cruising first one way then another allowed each eye to scrutinize in turn. The antelope froze in place, only their eyes tracked the meandering fish.

The shadow slowed, then hung motionless, her body curved in an arc, head and tail lowered—the defiant attack stance of her kind. Her cold, unblinking eye peered from beneath the water. The antelope peered back. Both sensed danger, but both were too fascinated to turn back. Neither one moved. All was quiet and still except for the murmuring water and the distant night sounds. The stand-off was finally broken by a single, curious antelope advancing a few hesitant steps. It paused in mid-step, ears forward, eyes shining. The dark shadow turned to meet him. The pronghorn's nostrils flared. Genuine fear was rising in him now, in spite of his curiosity.

In this position Naska could not see, but other more acute senses compensated. Her body felt the change in water pressure. Sensitive pores surrounding her mouth tasted the water. The tingling of these senses was her warning, but she wasn't quick enough. Her world exploded. The pronghorn struck with slashing hooves. He felt his first strike hit, then searing pain gripped his left front leg. He turned and leapt to the river bank. The others, as if one, instantly followed.

The herd left the river valley, trotting toward the rising morning star, now above the high prairie hills to the east. One limped, streaming blood from a deep gash to its front leg.

The pronghorn's slashing attack had cut deep, narrowly missing Naska's spine. Her reaction had been fast: a violent counter attack followed by a darting retreat. She left tasting blood.

The fight was brief but the effects devastating. Naska's needlelike sharp teeth had torn flesh as she shook her massive head from side to side. The pronghorn's small hooves, honed to a fine edge by climbing the rocky high ground, cut and crushed. Naska was lucky to be alive.

She retreated to the safety of deep water where, unmoving for many days, she nursed her wounds.

As she hovered, death close at hand, the river spoke to her again. "My riddles are written in your colours and patterns, in the coiled shell of the water snail and in the advance and retreat of my morning mist. All is there for those who seek. The willows know and bow before the river winds. I am as the veins of their stems and that of the animals. My sisters both young and old bring life to the land in the endless cycle of wind and water. We are ancient and honour only ice mountain and his creator. My father feels the deep stirrings of growth again. His advance will come soon, with the passing of ten thousand cycles of the sun. Death is always close at hand, but you, my defiant one, will live to hunt again."

The cold water of winter revived her. For the remainder of her days, though, she wore a distinct crescent-shaped scar high upon her back.

The spring brought high, murky water. The great, restless river cut new channels and deep holes. Fish, both hunter and prey, sought the sanctuary of the river's deepest pools. A strange truce resulted. Clustered together in desperate, common survival they faced into the current, awaiting the river's ebb. They ignored one another, choosing not to eat until the peril passed. Overhead, the river carried a deadly cargo of uprooted trees and smaller debris. In another time the fish would welcome the shade and shelter of a beached river log, but for now the debris was an adversary to be avoided. The gentle river was showing its wrathful side.

Naska's strong body was rocked by the swirling water and her sensitive gills ached from the heavily silted water.

In time the river subsided. The fish returned to their former roles. Hunter stalked prey and sought the safety of weed beds and shallow water. Naska hunted with renewed vigor over a territory she now knew only by instinct. For the river bed had been forever changed by the river's rampage.

Just as the butterfly changes and renews itself in the cocoon so too did Saskatchewan in the cleansing flood of the early spring. Life more bounteous than before returned with the subsiding waters.

The spring also brought subtle but significant change. The fishes of the north moved south, and Naska challenged their invasion. Goldeye, pickerel and the odd wandering pike all bore the tell-tale wounds of Naska's wrath.

One day a new threat appeared. It was a creature she had never met before. It was big and moved slowly like a log carried by the current. Her other senses told her it was a living being.

At any other time her actions would have been predictable. But this intruder made her pause. It was bigger than she, much bigger. She approached slowly, her back arched and her broad tail making slow, deliberate sweeps. The stranger kept to its slow, steady course along the river bottom, unconcerned by her approach. Naska's fury rose. Her body tensed, then she shot out of the gloom in dauntless attack. Her jaws did not grip. The intruder was far too large. She came at it again and again. Her teeth broke on a craggy back. The fight was entirely her own. The giant fish did not fight back. Almost with contempt it seemed, the giant continued its fluid movement slowly and methodically down river.

Naska launched a final attack. By luck or misfortune she struck the giant's tail fin. She felt flesh tearing, then saw the huge fin sweeping toward her. A powerful blow stunned her. She recovered in time to witness the long tapering tail of Namew the sturgeon vanishing down river. Their chance encounter was over.

The ice mountain's rule had come and gone many times before Naska grew too tired for the hunt. The smaller fish grew bold and she found it hard to catch them. Almost in disdain they drifted by her jaws, only to dart away when she moved to attack. What once took but an instant was now painfully slow. Her lightning-quick reflexes were gone. Her meals became slow-moving crayfish and frogs. On her last hunts, in complete contempt, the little fish followed her, seeking the remains of what little food she could find but not swallow. Naska's body ached and she spent much more time in solitude on the river bottom. Here she awaited the return of the comforting voice of the river spirit, but no voice was heard.

The time came when the moon was full and no shining back was seen breaking the river's surface. The moon waned and the night creatures along the edge of the land and water felt safe.

The morning star was at its highest point and the eastern sky was bright with early dawn. The sun rose red and fairweather clouds of violet and gold floated across the sky.

Naska's movements were slowing. Her gills once flushed with red blood grew pale and sickly. She didn't know why, only instinct drew her from her hovering place to the weed bed. With painful effort she closed her tired mouth over a single water plant. Then with a turn of her massive head she pulled it free. Straining against the current, she carried this hard-won prize back to her chosen place. No prey had taken so much effort as this simple task.

She faced into the current for the final time. The rising sun now bathed the river bottom in a soft halflight. Only the dying remained. Her gills stopped moving. Her mouth opened and closed a final time, freeing the water plant. Her tired body shook with her death rattle. She briefly drifted with the current, then rose slowly toward the sun. One eye saw blackness, the other a brilliant broken circle of light.

The light grew in intensity. A bright light she would only see once filled her being. Then all was blackness.

Wind and current brought the limp corpse to the water's edge. It drifted to a sandbar where it rocked back and forth with the lapping waves. The birds of the air feasted. Before the coming of the next sunrise, mighty Naska's body was reduced to bones and a toothy, grinning skull.

The night creatures, once timid of her mere approach, now rejoiced in her death. And so began a night of steady tatoo, celebrating the end of their once formidable foe. The frogs croaked together of a great victory, but theirs was not a valid boast. Only death had won.

In the spring the rushing water swept the bones along the river bottom where they collected in a shallow river hollow. Swirling silt covered them. A stand of water plants began to grow thick and lush from the calcium-rich sediment.

Along the wandering river, in the back water of a shallow place, small fish—the survivors of uncountable hatchlings—flittered among weeds, pursuing water bugs and minute creatures. Others much larger but no older, stalked tadpoles. They all feared the deep water where the larger fish lurked ever hungry for a meal of their kind. In time, the pull of instinct or perhaps destiny called the bold one to the deep, alluring water. She paused at a lush stand of water plants and hovered beside it. The water-filtered sun, moving in zebra-like patterns over her back, shone on a curious crescent-shaped birth mark. The singing river called her in the soft rustle of the water weeds and in the gurgle and murmur of water pouring around the few scattered boulders breaking the glassy surface.

The bold one swam deeper, down a sandy decline, past the last of the weed bed, and into the unknown reaches of the deep calling river.

Easy Afternoon, Lorne Fineday

ABOUT THE AUTHORS

Maria Campbell

Maria Campbell was born in northwest Saskatchewan, the oldest of eight children. When her mother died, Maria had to quit school to help her father, a Metis trapper, look after the other children.

As soon as she could write, Maria was writing stories and poems, "because there were things I was thinking that I couldn't tell anyone because they were too busy and also because it was in English and my grandmothers, who were the only ones who had time to listen to me, couldn't understand English."

Her first book, *Halfbreed*, was written because "I had a whole lot of stuff inside me that I had to write to find out who I was, to heal myself."

Riel's People and *People of the Buffalo* were written later when Maria discovered how hard it was for her own children to find books about their history. *Little Badger and the Fire Spirit* was her first piece of fiction.

Maria has travelled extensively in Canada and the United States, conducted many drama and writers workshops in Native communities, been writer-in-residence at the University of Alberta and for Persephone Theatre in Saskatoon.

She now lives at Gabriel's Crossing in Batoche, Saskatchewan, and is devoting most of her time to drama. "One of the reasons I like drama," she explains, "is that it, like storytelling, involves the exchange of energy between the storyteller and audience."

Peter Deranger

Peter Deranger lives in Regina, but comes from Uranium City. While living in the North, Peter was active in the anti-uranium movement. He is also one of the founders of the Native Youth movement in Canada, and has worked in various capacities in Canada and the United States for the betterment of his people.

Peter is a journalist and an oral storyteller. He is presently working on a novel and a collection of short stories.

Harvey Knight

Harvey was born in 1951, somewhere in the middle, he says, of a family of nine kids. He lived his first 12 years on the Muskoday Reservation, Saskatchewan. Then his father got a job with Indian Affairs and the family moved to Duck Lake, Kamsack and eventually Saskatoon.

In 1980, while living in Winnipeg, Harvey founded *Masenayegun* (which means "written record of a story"), a community newspaper which focussed on local, provincial and national economic, political and social issues. During his three years with *Masenayegun*, the monthly tabloid built up a circulation of 10,000. It has just recently announced that, due to lack of funding, publication must cease.

95

In 1983, Harvey came to Saskatoon as assistant editor for the *Saskatchewan Indian*. He became editor, only to lose the job when funds were cut and the magazine folded.

At that point, Harvey decided to go to university, "to explore forms of literature and the development of literature itself." He is now in his second year at the University of Saskatchewan and plans to pursue whatever profession will allow him to develop his writing skills.

Harvey is married and has three children.

Jordan Henry Wheeler

Born in Victoria in 1964, Jordan spent the first seven years of his life basking in the green wilderness of Vancouver Island. In 1972 his mother, writer/broadcaster Bernelda Wheeler, accepted a full-time job with CBC Winnipeg and since then Jordan has been, reluctantly, a prairie boy.

With early aspirations to be a journalist, Jordan began writing columns while still in high school. In 1982, he graduated from Tech Voc High School in Winnipeg. Since then, he has been to Indonesia on a student exchange program, and has worked as a vacuum cleaner salesman, a communications trainee at the First Nations Confederacy, and a production assistant with O'Meara Productions Ltd.

It was in Indonesia that Jordan decided he wanted to write fiction and there, in January–February 1983, he wrote his first major story, while lying on a white sand beach just north of the equator.

Wes Fineday

Wes is from the Sweetgrass Reservation, Saskatchewan. He comes from a family of oral storytellers and hereditary chiefs.

Wes has travelled extensively in western Canada, collecting stories and learning the craft of storytelling. Wes is also a poet and song-writer. He is presently working on the second draft of his first novel.

In addition to his writing, Wes has become deeply involved in issues related to Native people and the legal system.

Bernelda Winona Wheeler

Bernelda was born in the Qu'Appelle Valley, Saskatchewan in 1937, third living child of Colin and Clara Pratt of the Gordon's Reserve. Bernelda was brought up on the reserve until the age of nine, when the family moved to the northern Manitoba mining community of Herb Lake and then Churchill.

Bernelda began writing in grade school and began broadcasting as a teenager over CHFC in Fort Churchill.

After marrying and moving to B.C., she worked as a producer of short, weekly programs for CJAV in Port Alberni, hosted programs, began freelancing for Our Native

Land (CBC) in 1970 and wrote a column for the weekend supplement of the *Alberni Valley Times*.

Having separated in 1971, Bernelda moved to Winnipeg in 1972 to join Our Native Land as full-time story editor. She remained with the program for 10 years as host, story producer, producer and writer/broadcaster.

Bernelda has had items on Sunday Morning, Identities, As It Happens and Morningside on CBC and has been a columnist for *The New Nation* and *Indian Record*. She was nominated for an ACTRA award for best documentary in radio, and presented with a special award by the Winnipeg Broadcast Awards in 1982 for her contribution to Native programming in Canada.

Bernelda also has her LPN and has worked at the hospital in Port Alberni and as a school nurse at the Alberni Indian School. She is presently working as a rehabilitation counsellor for the Alcoholism Foundation of Manitoba, but writing, broadcasting and narrating in her spare time.

Priscilla Settee

Priscilla makes her home in Prince Albert, Saskatchewan, but her roots are in Cumberland House. She has travelled to many parts of the world and lived for a time in Mexico and Peru.

Priscilla is a teacher. She received her education degree from the University of Guelph. While doing her internship in Cumberland House, she did meet a special little girl called Phoebe.

Priscilla is deeply committed to the struggles of Native people, especially in the area of children and education.

Darlene R. Frenctte

Darlene was born in 1949 in Prince Albert, Saskatchewan. She attended Westmount School and Bedford Road Collegiate in Saskatoon. She is presently studying political science at the University of Saskatchewan.

Her first writing experience came in the summer of 1983 at a workshop conducted by Maria Campbell. That fall she took a second-year writing class from Lewis Horne at the U of S and the following year a Canadian fiction class from Elizabeth Brewster.

Darlene's father is Cree and her mother Ukrainian. The family is connected to the Scottish Sutherland family from One Arrow Reserve, which is adjacent to, and shares in the colourful history of, the Batoche area in Saskatchewan.

Through her marriage, Darlene has been able to add to her children's cultural heritage French, Dutch, English and Welsh strains. "My three children draw on the rich fabric of these cultural backgrounds. They are truly homogeneous world citizens. And they are the toughest judges of my stories."

Darlene has two full brothers: Ben, 30, holds a Bachelor of Music degree, specializing in classical guitar; Chuck, 33, searches for his vision.

John Cuthand

John Cuthand was born in Prince Albert, Saskatchewan in 1953. His father, an Anglican minister, was transferred from Indian mission to Indian mission across western Canada. This exposed young Cuthand to a variety of Indian cultures, from the Swampy Cree to the Blackfoot Confederacy to his people, the Plains Cree.

In 1974, after finishing high school and a series of odd jobs, John wrote an angry rebuttal to a Canadian politician's remarks about Indians. That landed him a job with the newspaper he had written to. Ten years later, and after working his way into the editorship of several Indian newspapers, John continues to write newspaper articles and has recently started writing a history of the Plains Cree.

John's stories and poems reflect three centuries of remembered Cree family history. He comes from a family of storytellers, legend-weavers, mystics and war chiefs. Their stories and his own experiences are the constant theme of his written works.

John Cuthand married Eileen Kinequon of the Daystar Reserve in 1984. They are expecting their first child in May, 1985.